About the Author

Amanda Mitchison grew up in Scotland. She has travelled widely. Her first job as a journalist was on the Egyptian Gazette in Cairo and she later worked as a radio reporter for the Vatican in Rome. She now writes for British newspapers and lives in Bristol with her husband and two sons.

AMANDA MITCHISON

CORGI BOOKS

CROG

A CORGI BOOK 978 0 552 56853 1

First published in Great Britain by Corgi,
an imprint of Random House Children's Publishers UK
A Random House Group Company

This edition published 2015

1 3 5 7 9 10 8 6 4 2

Penguin Random House is committed to a sustainable future for our business, our readers
and our planet. This book is made from Forest Stewardship Council® certified paper.

Set in 11/18pt Hoefler Text by Falcon Oast Graphic Art Ltd.

RANDOM HOUSE CHILDREN'S PUBLISHERS UK
61–63 Uxbridge Road, London W5 5SA

www.**randomhousechildrens**.co.uk
www.**totallyrandombooks**.co.uk
www.**randomhouse**.co.uk

Addresses for companies within The Random House Group Limited can be found at:
www.randomhouse.co.uk/offices.htm

THE RANDOM HOUSE GROUP Limited Reg. No. 954009

A CIP catalogue record for this book is available from the British Library.

Printed and bound in Great Britain by CPI Group (UK) Ltd, Croydon, CR0 4YY

cròg, -òige: hand, clutch, claw or fist.

Làn mo chròige de'n òr bhuidhe:
My fist full of yellow gold.

From Edward Dwelly's Gaelic–English Dictionary

CHAPTER 1

Sometimes you just have to get out. Wilf felt stale and bored. His thumbs ached from the console and he'd drunk too many sports drinks with 'go faster' stripes on the side. A packet of BBQ-rib crisps was repeating on him.

So he went outside. But outside was stale and bored too. He trudged along the river, with a grey sky overhead and the tower blocks of London tilting down at him. He skirted a rotten gangway that melted down into the water. Underfoot it was horrible. That was the thing about Wapping: neither dry ground nor water; just pebbles and slime and mud. Mud and builders' boards. And more mud.

The Thames slid slowly past, a few fluffed-up ducks on the surface. One duck had a trail of fluffed-up ducklings behind her.

Wilf stared at the black water. Lucky ducks – able to fluff up like that. He couldn't do that – he didn't have feathers; he didn't have much in the way of clothes either – just his biker's jacket with the aluminium foil in the lining to trick security sensors. He didn't do hats or scarves. And he only half did jeans – they were hanging down around his crotch, so his bum was freezing.

Soon he'd had enough. A small flight of steps brought him up onto the road. He scanned the landscape for a good warm newsagent's. He needed a cigarette, or at least a packet of sweets. But there was nothing.

He walked on, taking an underpass and coming up in a clearing among the tower blocks. The area was paved, with a few shrubs and a fountain in the centre. On the far side stood the museum.

Did the museum have a café? At least it'd be warm. And it would look good – give him something to talk about when Mr Robertson asked him if he'd been spending his time productively.

Wilf crossed the square and entered through a revolving glass door.

The museum had fourteen interconnecting rooms, but no café. And there was nowhere to sit down – the only chair was taken by a snoozing security guard, a great sausage of a man with little bracelets of fat at his wrists. Wilf was the only person there – the place was silent, and the rustle of his aluminium foil sounded loud.

He wandered through into the first room.

Wilf quite liked museums. Even if the exhibits were

pointless, the security arrangements were always interesting. And this museum had recently had a glossy makeover. There was two-centimetre-thick reinforced glass, high-output alarm sirens, micro movement detectors with small blinking red lights. It must've cost a bomb.

Wilf turned his attention to the display cases, which mostly, according to the blurb in the entrance hall, housed finds from Britain's coastal waters. And there was an awful lot of stuff – everyone who'd ever crossed the Thames seemed to have thrown something in. Even policemen were guilty of littering: there was an entire case given over to old watermarked truncheons.

As he went from room to room, the displays receded back through the centuries: fragments of china, broken clay pipes, old buttons, an Anglo-Saxon bone comb with most of the teeth missing. What could you do with a toothless comb? It was all rubbish really. Ancient rubbish.

Wilf moved on, passing bronze helmets and swords. He stumbled into the next room, only half noticing a large red banner overhead mentioning new acquisitions. Then something startled him. He stopped, and he looked.

Standing in the very middle of the polished floor was a large glass case. And inside this case was just one thing – a small wooden bowl with a thin, serrated gold rim and a small chip on one side. That was all. There was nothing else – only this one beautiful bowl.

Wilf walked up to the case quietly, as if the bowl were listening. He read the label, which said that this was a very recent find from an excavation on the shores of Loch Etive, on the west coast of Scotland, led by the late Professor John Williams of Glasgow University. Below was a small newspaper cutting: the bowl, it seemed, had arrived at the museum that very morning. So hardly anyone had seen it – possibly just Wilf and a few museum staff; and, of course, the late Professor Williams. And why call him 'late'? That was stupid. The dead were dead, weren't they? Not *late*.

Wilf stood very still. As he rested his gaze on the bowl, he felt a thick wave of silence break over him. The wood was darker than mahogany and very smooth; it had a silky sheen. There was no decoration except for the gold rim and the natural markings of the wood – three very faint growth rings. The rings banded the bowl like tropics around a globe; the wood must have come from the very centre of the tree.

Wilf studied the bowl. Yet, just for a moment, the bowl seemed to evade him and he caught a glimmer of two round, deep-set eyes – his eyes, of course – reflected back at him in the glass. He must get more sleep.

He looked again.

The bowl really was the perfect size. And the shape was just right too: the sides were not too steep, and the bottom not too shallow. If he were out walking in the mountains and he knelt down and cupped his hands to drink from a stream, then this was exactly the size of bowl his hands would make. And the little chip on one side was just like one of the cracks there would be in between his fingers.

This bowl . . . Simple. Beautiful. Perfect.

And it said *Take me!*

His pulse quickened. He felt alive. The afternoon no longer stretched out before him. Now he had something he wanted to do, even if it meant disappointing Mr Robertson.

Wilf looked hard at the bowl.

The bowl glowed back at Wilf.

Take me!

This wasn't his first time. A lot of things in life said *Take me!* to Wilf. And Wilf, being a kindly soul, usually tried to oblige. Before his last conviction he'd liberated countless car radios and items of jewellery as well as some top-of-the-range vehicles.

But with this bowl, it was different. This was not remotely sensible. The bowl would be completely traceable. Zero resale value. Yet this was something he simply had to do.

Should he? Shouldn't he?

It wasn't his fault. The bowl just seemed to pull him in.

Wilf's eyes flitted around the display case.

Hold on!

The little red light of the motion detector was no longer flashing. He checked the security camera in the top corner of the room and could clearly see that the internal shutter was down. This too had been deactivated!

That was odd. Maybe the system was still being tested, or having a few start-up glitches. But it was as good as an invitation. Why was he waiting?

For just a millisecond he wrestled with his conscience. *Wrestle* wasn't really the right word. For Wilf was a big, tall Year Eight, and his conscience was a mere puny, knock-kneed Year Six. So no contest really.

Wilf glanced behind him, thrust his hand into his jeans pocket and brought out a small silver pen. He quickly unscrewed the top. Inside was a miniature carborundum-tipped drill. He pressed the drill head against the glass and slid back the release switch on the motor.

The drill made a scrinching noise as it bored its way through the glass. Even though he had to press hard,

Wilf found himself smiling. This really *was* a good gadget.

He drew the drill round, making a circle in the glass. His breathing was completely steady, his movements fluid. He felt light, as if he were dancing.

He pushed the circle of glass into the case, shutting his eyes and wincing as he did so. No alarm sounded. No siren. There was no stopping him now. And he even had time for a little joke. He took up the drill again and added two more little circles up above, so that the hole gained Mickey Mouse ears.

Wilf thrust his hand through the hole and, in a soundless instant, grabbed the bowl. A little surge of fire crept up his spine.

The bowl was as light as a biscuit.

He opened his jacket and slipped it into the largest of his internal pockets. The bowl had no electronic marker tags, so for once he didn't need the foil lining he'd so carefully sewn in. All the same, the aluminium might protect the bowl if he had to do a runner.

He didn't need to run. And he never ran, not if he didn't have to. Instead he strode briskly – very briskly – towards the exit.

He was smiling when he came to the main hall. His fingertips, his face, his body, his mind – everything tingled. He felt fantastic! He always felt fantastic when he'd turned a good trick. Particularly if he'd carried it out with style. And today had been a polished performance – the Mickey Mouse ears were such a nice touch.

As he passed by, the fat security guard snuffled in his sleep.

There was still no alarm. Still no siren. It was all *too* easy.

Wilf pushed at the revolving door, and saw two men in suits hurrying up to the front steps. He went in, and at the same moment, they entered from the other side. He pushed; they pushed. The mechanism jammed and the turnstile halted.

And so now Wilf was stuck in his glass cubicle. A fly in amber. The two men in the other cubicle looked thin and wiry and not entirely clean. Yet the suits were sharp and clearly expensive.

One of the men was smoking a cigarillo. He pushed against the door – and Wilf saw the muscle down the side of his face harden with frustration. There was something not quite right about the men. They were not museum sorts. Too watchful. Too pent up. Slightly creepy. Not normal mortals. Security detail for some Russian oligarch? Mercenaries? Police? And why a cigarillo? No proper person smoked those.

Wilf looked out at the square. The sky had darkened

and hail was bouncing on the paving stones. That was quick – he'd only been in the museum a few minutes.

The turnstile still wasn't moving; he was stuck. Wilf took out his mobile and fired off a quick text to Fred, a useful friend and rival with whom he kept up a little tally. He tapped, *Dun a quality job! Way out of yr league!* and pinged it off.

Suddenly uncomfortable, he lifted his gaze. The two men were staring at him through the glass partition. So Wilf looked down at his feet, and at their feet. The man nearest to him was wearing shoes made of an exotic leather covered in small, regular bumps. What was it? Peccary? Toad? Iguana?

If only the door would move! Wilf focused on the shoes. Expensive, and vulgar. He knew the men were still looking at him. But why shouldn't they look at him?

Now, he could tell, they were *examining* him. And he wasn't a museum exhibit. Or a museum sort, either.

Wilf was only one metre away from them. Only one metre. He *must not* sweat!

Scared? He had to face them.

He turned and gave them a wide, sleepy smile. The man furthest from him – he had dark hair sweeping back from his forehead with a badger's streak of white to one side – lowered his gaze to fiddle with an extraordinary round, shiny silver thing that looked like a mobile; it opened and closed like a starfish. The nearer man – hard grey eyes and a stubby snout of a nose – went on staring. *I'd call him 'Snout'*, thought Wilf. *Badger and Snout*.

Wilf's mobile gave a tiny electronic cough, as if it were clearing its throat. And at the same time, with a judder, the revolving door started moving round again.

As Wilf stepped out into the square he caught the sweet, slightly musty smell of cigar smoke. The hail beat down on his shoulders.

Strange how the weather had changed – you shouldn't get hail in May. Strange too about the alarm being switched off. And why were the security cameras not working? Why the sleeping warden? And those men . . . Police? But he'd heard no sirens, no alarms. And they'd come too quickly – normally you had at least ten minutes before anyone showed up. And he'd been so near them he could see the pores in their skin. That wasn't right. Not right at all.

For Wilf, all this strangeness came together in one most unusual sensation – a jolt of fear. And the fear pinched him in the knees, so that on the bottom step he stumbled.

But he was curious. He wanted to know more. He needed to find a vantage point and see who these men were. Of course, later he wondered why he didn't just go straight home. But he didn't. He always had to go too far, always had to push his luck. Mr Robertson was right. That was, and always would be, his downfall.

CHAPTER 2

Wilf took the nearest exit, heading east out of the square. Once out of sight of the museum, he turned into a hotel car park, ducked under the barriers, and doubled back to where the road joined the far end of the square. At the corner, he hid behind some dustbins. The hail pinged loudly – as if a giant were drumming his fingernails on the metal lids.

From here Wilf could see the museum entrance – but he was not too dangerously near. Or so he thought.

He peered round the bins. Nothing. Nobody at the entrance. Nobody on the steps. No sound of an alarm. No sirens. No police cars.

The revolving door flicked round, and out came the two men. For a second they stood there. One of them, Snout, scanned the square, while Badger looked down at the silver thing in his hand.

Wilf's phone gave another tiny cough.

Badger nodded towards the bins. He and Snout leaped down the steps three at a time. They hit the square running.

Wilf clambered out from behind the bins. He dashed back down the road, now slippery with melting hail.

They weren't particularly big men, but they were fit. And in an open space they'd outrun him in minutes.

He vaulted the barricade into the hotel car park. He passed a nice lime-green Jaguar XF Concept – no time now to take it. And the colour would stand out.

He didn't have much time. He had to think of something. *Think!*

But he couldn't think, so he just ran.

Now they were not far behind. Not far at all.

At the end of the car park there was a bicycle with its security chain looped round some metal fencing. That wouldn't take too long. He got out his favourite gadget, flicked on the motor and pressed the drill bit down against the padlock. The drill swivelled and swirled, going round slower and slower. It was running out of juice.

Wilf breathed angrily. Definitely *not* his favourite gadget any more.

The drill came to a stop.

He glanced up. Badger was at the barrier, but Snout was in the car park, running towards him.

Maybe sixty metres away? Or less.

Wilf tried the drill once more. Dead.

Forty metres now. And he was still tinkering away like an idiot!

He tugged at the padlock. Maybe the drill had already done enough damage? For a moment the lock juddered. Then it clicked open.

He pulled at the chain; it caught against the railings. Again he tugged, and this time it came free.

Snout was only five metres away now, and putting on a last catch-up spurt of speed. There was only one thing now that Wilf could do. With a force he didn't know he had, he threw the chain and it flew through the air, a snake of metal that hit the legs of the running man.

Those few shavings of a second while Snout groaned and fell were just long enough. Wilf swung his leg over the bike. Head ducked down, he pedalled like crazy. He was away! Through the car-park entrance and on up the road, weaving round cars and bucking the bike up onto pavements and down again.

Soon his hands were freezing; the hail was still pelting down, stinging his face and setting off car alarms. The bike seat was far too low, but Wilf didn't care.

He came out onto a main road. Had he lost them?

He looked back. No one behind him. But he knew it wasn't over. Police and security detail always had wheels. They'd be making for their unmarked car. Maybe they were already taking a loop round and charging back down the road towards him. Or maybe they were lying in wait.

Up ahead, a silver Mercedes suddenly stopped just before the roundabout. Cars were beeping and swerving round it.

Wilf braked too. He could just make out two men sitting in the front of the car. Were they *his* men, Snout and Badger? It seemed likely, but he couldn't be sure, as his view was blocked by the neck rests. Luckily, however, the office block to his right had a mirrored front. Wilf looked in the glass – it presented a perfect profile of the silver Mercedes. But the reflection showed an *empty* silver Mercedes. There was no driver, even though the car was moving, and no one in the passenger seat.

What was going on? A second ago he'd seen the backs of their heads, and now there was no one. People don't just disappear. And cars don't drive themselves – even a Mercedes.

Maybe it was the hail? Or the mirrored glass wasn't right? Or his nerves were getting the better of him? But there was no time now to worry about anything. Wilf made for the pavement and, standing on the pedals, juddered down the steps to the underpass. The tunnel stank of urine but he didn't care. He just sped on through and swerved up the ramp on the far side.

He came up on the east side of the roundabout. Instantly horns blared and brakes screamed and the Mercedes sped through the traffic, cutting across cars and bumping slow drivers out of the way. Now Wilf didn't need any mirrored office front. He could see only too well. It *was* Badger and Snout in the front seats. Badger was driving straight towards Wilf – straight *at* him. The car would surely break the railings like matchsticks.

To one side Wilf saw a gap between the buildings and a line of bollards cordoning off a pedestrian precinct. He dived between the bollards, passing café tables and rows of plants in big pots.

He was riding high now. Grinning inanely, he thanked God for the bollards and for the bad weather that had emptied the precinct of toddlers and slow-moving old ladies with little dogs, all of whom he would certainly have ploughed straight into.

Wilf raced on. He came to a narrow alley littered with piles of cardboard boxes and huge metal crates. He'd taken this route several times before and he glanced up. The metal barrier at the far end was down, blocking access to vehicles. So no nasty surprises.

Yet.

His phone coughed again. He glanced up. At the end of

the alley he could see the silver nose of a car that had just pulled up by the kerb.

The Mercedes.

He swivelled the handlebars round. Back he went, down the alley, and left past the café. He threw the bike down by the bollards, and flattened himself against the side of the building. He looked out. No silver Mercedes.

Yet.

Instead there was a black taxi with its FOR HIRE light on. Just waiting to save him. Only he wasn't the first to spot it – a middle-aged man in a suit had marched out the café and was nearly at the cab. But that wasn't a problem. Wilf ran up and tapped him lightly on the arm.

'Excuse me, sir,' said Wilf in his party best voice, 'but you've left your card at the till.'

The man gave a start of surprise, thanked him and turned back towards the café.

Wilf got into the taxi. 'Canary Wharf, please.'

The taxi driver took a road that bridged West India Quay. He was driving above two grey-green blocks of water.

Wilf sank back into the upholstery. They'd be onto him again soon. Canary Wharf was the right place, for he knew all its emergency staircases and anonymous concrete backways. He'd confuse them. Split them up.

Funny that he'd not heard a siren yet. These men were smart. How did they know he was going to take that alleyway?

His mobile gave another little cough . . . *That's* how they knew. The mobile. They'd been tracking his movements. *They* weren't stupid. *He* was stupid.

He wound down the window. Still no silver Mercedes. But there was no time now to take out the SIM card. He just flung the phone out of the window. It was quite a drop down into the quay and Wilf heard no splash, nothing.

Just a tired sigh from inside the cab.

The cab driver looked at Wilf reproachfully in the rear-view mirror. 'You don't have any money on you, do you?'

Wilf looked shocked. 'Of course I do!'

Of course he didn't.

CHAPTER 3

Wilf was still half asleep. The light hurt. He kept his eyes closed. Already he knew that something was wrong.

There was a smell. A ripe, sewagey smell. A smell that might be OK on a farm. Only Wilf didn't live on a farm. Wilf lived in central London. He was in bed, at home in his father's luxury flat on the sixth floor of Wilmot Towers.

So something was not right.

Wilf woke up a little more. Eh? What was this? He was not alone. There was a presence in the corner of his room. A presence that he could just tell was watching him. Who was it? A friend on the run?

The presence made a squelching sound.

Then it coughed.

Wilf opened one eye. Crouched there was a muddy, bedraggled boy dressed in a brown jerkin. He had skin the colour of an old pub ceiling and brown hair that hung down in long, wet tendrils. He was stroking the window-pane. Wilf shut his eyes again. He felt outraged. It was yet another waif and stray. How on earth had he snuck into the building? What was Jenkins thinking letting someone like that through? *And* at this hour? And why did they always have to come to *him*?

Wilf felt on the ground by his bed for a packet of cigarettes. The packet was empty. What a rubbish morning. He rolled over towards the wall. But that was a bad move – for his back and thighs ached horribly from all the pedalling yesterday.

And now there was this strange boy. And the smell.

'Here it rests,' said the boy in the corner. He had a most peculiar accent.

'Leave me alone,' moaned Wilf. 'I just want some sleep.'

'I slept the sleep of three thousand years,' said the stranger.

'Yeah, yeah,' murmured Wilf. 'Course you did.' How *had* he got in? He stank and he talked rubbish. It was so annoying – the least he could do was shut up.

But the voice was quite firm. 'I slept the sleep of three thousand years. And now I have wakened. And here it rests.'

'*What* rests?' asked Wilf.

'I failed afore. I must not fail again,' said the boy tonelessly.

Wilf turned back. The boy was definitely a weirdo. Around his neck – and the skin there looked horribly pulled out of shape – hung a length of soggy rope. What was he trying to prove? Nobody used rope on a job. What was the point when you could usually get in on the ground floor? And anyway, polypropylene cord, available in any mountaineering shop, was so much lighter and stronger. And why, for that matter, tie the rope around your neck? One little fall, the rope catches and you'd be a goner. What an amateur!

'That rope . . . What's the rope for?' said Wilf.

The boy winced.

'And what makes you think you've been asleep for three thousand years? We've all slept in after a hard night, but *three thousand years?*' Wilf regretted the question immediately – it was always easier not to get involved, especially with strange people.

'I know,' the boy insisted. 'I know.'

'And who are you, anyway?'

'Crog.' He said the word with a slight croak on the 'o'.

'Craw? Like what a crow does?'

'Nay. Crog.' Another croak. 'My birth name is Crog.'

'Oh. I'm Wilf. Well, Wilfred really. Wilfred MacGregor,' said Wilf.

'Wil-fred,' repeated Crog bleakly. 'It is good to have a long name. It bodes well.'

There was a moment's silence while Wilf tried to think of a reply. He could say *Crog is a very nice name*, or *I'd like to be called Crog*. But then, why bother to lie? Why be polite before breakfast? And what *was* Crog doing here?

In his mind Wilf rummaged through the sad oddballs from his past. 'Did you once do a trick with me?'

Crog blinked back at him.

He tried again: 'A trick? A job? You know . . . Duh – a robbery?'

Crog shook his head.

'And how'd you get in?'

'I found myself here,' replied Crog.

'What do you mean *found yourself here*?' said Wilf sourly. 'What did you do? Fly in through the window?'

'The *window*?'

Wilf took a deep breath. That must be it – special needs. 'The window . . . You know, the hole in the wall that you are sitting beside.'

Crog tapped the glass. 'This? The hard air?'

'Yes.' Wilf narrowed his eyes. What was he on? 'It's called *glass*.'

'I may be rude as the sparrow, but my wits are whole,'

said Crog huffily. 'Just things here are new upon me.'

Wilf looked at him more closely. He was small, his eyes too big, his age hard to judge. He had two deep creases running from his nostrils down to the corners of his mouth. The skin was stretched tight over his cheekbones. And the accent was so odd. Scottish? Perhaps some tiny, faraway island?

'How old are you?' asked Wilf.

Crog shrugged.

'Are you twelve? Thirteen? A really, really small sixteen?'

Crog looked back blankly at him.

A little pool of muddy water with a few streaks of blood in it had formed around him, and a brown trickle was reaching out across the room. There was, Wilf realized, nothing more to say. Both boys watched the trickle as it made its way under the dirty football strip and round a chewing-gum wrapper. It was nearly at Wilf's bed when the door opened.

Wilf's twin sister Ishbel was in her running gear.

He pulled the bedclothes up over his head.

'Come on! You should be up by now. It's nearly ten.' Ishbel's nostrils flared. 'And *what* have you been eating?'

She caught sight of Crog and quickly looked him up and down.

'This is "Crog",' Wilf told her. 'I've never seen him before in my life.'

'Why did you let him in, then?' asked Ishbel.

'I didn't. He was here when I woke up. He says he has been asleep for three thousand years. Maybe he apparated.'

'Very funny,' she said flatly. Then she turned to Crog. 'Who are you? What exactly are you doing here?'

'I found and came to myself here,' he replied.

Ishbel rolled her eyes and turned to Wilf. 'This won't do. We can't have people just wandering in. The tenants' association should hold a security review.'

She inspected Crog again, this time more carefully. 'Crikey!' she exclaimed. 'What have you been doing? Look at your hands!' There was blood on Crog's fingers.

He looked sheepish.

'What you need, Crog,' said Ishbel, 'is a nice hot bath and something to eat.'

Crog smiled. His teeth were spectacular.

Wilf showed him the bathroom. Crog looked at the basins, the heated wall fittings, the Japanese self-warming toilet seat, the Jacuzzi bath in the shape of a giant clam. Most of Wilf's friends looked gobsmacked when they saw the bathroom. In fact they were gobsmacked by the whole apartment block, with its helipads and the base-ment swimming pool and gym complex. But they were always particularly gobsmacked by the bathroom.

Nobody, however, had ever been quite as gobsmacked as Crog. He gazed at everything, and then at Wilf.

'Here are some towels,' said Wilf.

Crog looked at him, puzzled. Wilf, feeling uncomfort-able, turned away. He caught sight of his reflection in the mirror above the wash basin and it showed up his face in all its morning unloveliness. He checked over the tally of flaws. His freckles, which had come out with the start of spring, even though the sun had stayed away all sea-son. And there were slight sores at the corners of his mouth, due to him never knowingly eating a vegetable. The overlapping front teeth told another story: ortho-dontists are only human too, and after the umpteenth missed appointment, Mr Riley, like so many other con-cerned professionals in Wilf's life, had finally given up.

Wilf comforted himself with the thought that at least Crog's face was worse. He looked in the mirror again. But there was no Crog, not even the back of his head. Wilf stood stock-still – this was like that strange moment yesterday, when he'd looked in the mirrored shop front and those men sitting in the Mercedes had vanished . . .

Wilf swivelled round. Crog had crouched down and

was sniffing the perfumed steam coming from a small floor vent. Was he simply so low down that he was out of sight of the mirror?

Wilf didn't quite know what to think, or do. 'Look, Crog,' he said. 'This is the bath. I'll just run it for you.'

He activated the touchscreen panel, adjusted the light settings to 'warm candlelight' and tapped in some jazz. Crog's mouth opened and his head bobbed slightly. He had the same fixed stare that Wilf had seen before on newborn babies and bored-out-of-their-minds security guards.

And he showed no signs of getting undressed.

'You take your clothes off,' said Wilf loudly and slowly. He didn't want to look at Crog's hands too closely. 'You get in the bath and then you rub this stuff – it's called soap – into your skin. Then you wash it off.'

'Where is your knife?' asked Crog.

'My knife? We don't keep knives in the bathroom,' said Wilf. 'What d'you need a knife for?'

Crog pulled at the front of his jerkin as if trying to part the seam. And then Wilf understood. Crog's top had no zip, no buttons, no ties. He had been *sewn into his clothes*. Wilf opened a drawer. All he could find was a pair of manicure scissors and he showed Crog how they worked.

Wilf watched him play with the scissors, snapping them in the air, trying them against the side of his hand,

and cutting a nick in his chin. Where *did* this creature come from? He'd probably never used a toilet, either.

'You pee and you poo down this hole . . .' Wilf sat down on the seat for a moment and made a straining face. He pulled off a piece of toilet paper and made wiping motions, then pressed the flush. Crog's face lit up.

Wilf turned the extractor fan to maximum and then left Crog to his own devices. As he closed the bathroom door, he heard the toilet flush. As he went into the kitchen, the toilet flushed again. As he sat down, the toilet flushed for a third time.

Ishbel was doing her stretching exercises. She'd already taken off her wet trainers and had neatly stuffed them with newspaper.

'Well?' she said. 'This is really odd. What's he doing here. And why?'

'I dunno. I don't like it, either. It's not my fault,' said Wilf.

'I disagree. It's sure to be some little intrigue of yours. You really have landed us with a right one this time.' As she spoke, Ishbel bent over, touching the floor with the flat of her hands. Her head was upside down now.

'Can't you talk to me the right way up?' said Wilf.

'I like to fill my time productively. Who is he, your little friend . . . your new human pet?'

'He's not a pet. His name is Crog.'

'Crog? That's not a proper name – that's a sound you make with your mouth.' Ishbel straightened up and added, 'Did you check him for matches?'

'What d'you mean?'

'Remember that little arsonist with the piercings you picked up? Now, *he* was very expensive.'

'Crog's not like that,' said Wilf, though he didn't know why he was defending someone he'd barely met. 'He probably doesn't know what matches are. Or windows. He doesn't know how old he is. He doesn't even know what a flushing toilet is.'

'So I can hear,' said Ishbel.

'Don't you get it? *He's never seen a toilet before!*'

'And he's a terrible colour,' added Ishbel. 'It's like he's never seen the light of day before. What does he eat? I bet he lives off bogofs, and onion rings. Where does he come from?'

'I dunno,' said Wilf. 'And you are *such* a snob.'

'Sewers maybe? He is just like one of those weird white squidgy animals you find in caves. Pass us an orange.'

Wilf passed the orange. 'Honest, Ishie, it's a mystery. He was here when I woke up. He can't have climbed out of a remand centre with that rope. Did you see his hands? They're all bloody.'

'At least his blood's red, not green,' said Ishbel.

'Ishie! Be serious. How d'you think he got in?'

She was removing the orange peel in one long ringlet. 'How do I know? He can't have come through the ground floor – not with Jenkins and the scanners. Maybe he climbed up the side of the building . . . Maybe he's got suckers on his paws . . . Bit of a cheek, though, isn't it?'

'But where's he from?' pressed Wilf. 'He says he's three thousand years old.'

Ishbel gave a derisive snort. 'Yeah. I thought he might be from one of those re-enactment societies, but then I saw his teeth. Do you think he might be one of those "wild children" – you know, like they find in the jungle in Papua New Guinea.'

'There's not much jungle in E14.'

'What'll Dad say?' wondered Ishbel.

'Would he care? He never notices anything. Anyway, he's away for ages.'

Ishbel looked at the calendar on the wall. There was a line with DAD AWAY written on it that tracked the second half of May and the first four days of June.

'True enough,' she said. 'But clean the bathroom up after your little friend. He'll leave a scum ring in the bath. It's not fair on the maids.'

Wilf closed his eyes for a second. Trust Ishbel to think of scum rings. No poetry in her soul. Just scum rings. Hard to believe he'd shared a womb for nine whole months with somebody who thought about scum rings.

He put some bread in the toaster. And as he did so, memories of yesterday crowded into his mind – the chase, those men, that tricky little moment nipping away from the taxi driver. And Badger and Snout: where were they from? Not police – not with those shoes and that driving. Maybe some nasty little private offshoot. The telephone tracking device must be new security issue. How did they lock onto him?

Wilf did not have a good feeling about this.

'Ishie, you went out running this morning, didn't you?' He tried to sound casual.

'Yeah. I did. And?' said Ishbel without looking up.

'Notice anything unusual?'

'Like what?'

'Anything,' said Wilf.

'Well, Jenkins must really be losing his grip. He'd gone off to the loo or something, leaving the doors open. And the floor in the hallway was filthy. Mud everywhere. I don't know what Jenkins is playing at. That's when Crog must have snuck in.'

'I mean, something serious,' said Wilf.

'And that's not bad enough? What're you getting at?' asked Ishbel.

'Was there anyone, you know, out and about? Police? Security guards? That kind of thing?'

'No. There was just a diving team with dredging equipment. Must be another suicide.'

'Where?'

'West India Quay. It's a really inconsiderate way to top yourself. Costs the taxpayer millions.'

'Who was there? How many?' asked Wilf, just about keeping the quiver out of his voice.

'I didn't see any bodies,' replied Ishbel. 'Just two divers with little nets and bleepers and mobiles and stuff. What's the matter? You've gone all green. I never knew you were sensitive.'

Wilf was thinking: you don't look for bodies with little nets. They had bleepers. They were looking for a mobile phone. *His* mobile phone. Anyone can track you down if they've got your phone.

The sense of dread made him feel slightly floaty. How long had he got?

CHAPTER 4

Crog appeared at the kitchen door. He was dressed rather oddly in a pair of Wilf's tracksuit bottoms, a brightly coloured kaftan and the kind of sleeveless jacket war photographers use, full of little pockets and Velcro tags. He still had the rope dangling wetly around his neck. But he smelled better now, and gave off only a faint biological odour, like a warm ham sandwich.

'*What* are you wearing? That's Dad's photographer's waistcoat and it's far too big for you. And that top belonged to our mother!' said Wilf.

Crog stroked the kaftan and smiled. 'Like as to a rainbow.'

'It's good he's using it. Kaftans are quite retro,' said Ishbel. 'And I hate the way Dad hangs onto all her things . . . We can't keep them for ever.'

'All the same . . .' said Wilf. 'Wearing her old clothes, it's a bit like the dead walking again.'

Ishbel laughed uneasily and Crog crouched down in a corner of the kitchen. His eyes were following Ishbel's hamster, Gordon, who was having his morning run in his exercise ball. It skittered back and forth across the floor.

'Come and sit at the table.' Ishbel beckoned him over.

Crog seemed wary.

She rapped on the table impatiently. 'Crog! Off the ground please. Sit on a chair like a proper person. You're not a dog. Or a handbag.'

He climbed gingerly onto the chair, and crouched there with his knees up.

'What would you like for breakfast?' asked Ishbel.

'Blood?' said Crog hopefully.

'Sorry. We're out of blood,' she said flatly.

'Gruel?'

'We don't do gruel. We do cornflakes, toast and, on a good day, Cocoa Hooplas.'

Crog said nothing; his eyes still followed Gordon's ball back and forth.

'Make your mind up!' said Ishbel. 'And in case you thought otherwise, the hamster is not on the menu.'

'Uh . . . corncrakes,' said Crog uncertainly.

'Cornflakes *what*?'

'Sorry, Crog,' said Wilf. 'She's got a thing about manners. Just say *Cornflakes* please! That'll keep her happy.'

'Corncakes please,' intoned Crog.

Wilf opened the fridge to get the milk out. The maids had been shopping and it was full of cellophane packets of food, which Crog stared at with a glazed smile.

Wilf was about to hand him the packet of cornflakes but, remembering his experience in the bathroom, thought better of it. How would he know what was edible? What if he accidentally ate the packaging? Wilf took a bowl, poured in cornflakes and milk, and handed it to Crog.

Crog ate noisily, holding the bowl up close to his mouth. He had a cup of hot lemon and honey, two more helpings of cornflakes, and then Ishbel made him two rounds of toast. He remembered to say please every time, and he ate as if he hadn't eaten for three thousand years.

When he had finished, Crog sat crouched on his chair, stroking the window, staring down at the river and the road and the moving cars far below. He picked at his black, broken teeth with the end of a fork.

Wilf needed to clear his head, tidy his thoughts, tidy up after Crog. He pulled on jeans and a jumper and trainers and went into his father's dressing room. The door had been left open and he was relieved to find everything in order: the rows of neatly pressed shirts and jackets, and behind them the kilts and shiny-buttoned jackets that his father only ever wore for Burns Night suppers with other bankers. A drawer full of Highland regalia was slightly ajar. Wilf pushed it shut.

At the back of the room stood the two rails of his mother's clothes hanging in dry-cleaners' bags. His father hated her things being disturbed, and Crog had left the hanger and the plastic cover for the kaftan on the floor. Wilf picked them up. He felt slightly annoyed. Crog was taking a bit of a liberty removing her clothes without permission. But then, she wasn't there to ask, was she? She was long dead. So long dead that Wilf had no memory of her. Well, he had *something* – just the faintest echo of a hot, hazy day in a barley field somewhere in Scotland.

And now he took a liberty himself. He plunged forward between the rails, pushing the clothes aside. That was how it had been all those years ago. He had been so young that the barley had been taller than him and he had been pushing his way through, just as he was now pushing his way through the clothes bags.

Through the barley stalks, he could just see her up ahead in her bright yellow dress. And as he stumbled towards her, he heard her laugh, and she had picked him up into the sunlight and swirled him round in the air, and his cup of happiness had been full.

At the far end of the rail, Wilf grabbed the yellow

dress. He rucked up the plastic cover and buried his nose in the material. He hoped for a barley field on a summer's day, but he inhaled only mustiness.

He put down the dress quickly. It was sleeveless and dated. You didn't see people wearing yellow like that now – except possibly the Queen.

At least no one had seen him.

Wilf went into the bathroom. Breathing through his mouth, he examined the pile of clothes on the floor.

Where on earth had Crog come from?

There were no labels. And no washing instructions. Everything was hand-stitched, sometimes neatly, sometimes not. The trousers were leather and the jerkin was made of a very stiff material – maybe bark that had been flattened or stretched. There were some undergarments too – indescribable and brown. Using a towel, he picked everything up and placed it in a white plastic laundry bag. Then he went into the utility room, wrote *MacGregor* on the bag and put it down the chute on the pulley. What would the women in the basement laundry make of Crog's clothes? Maybe he could pretend they were for a school play.

When Wilf came back into the kitchen, he picked up the newspaper. But he couldn't read it – not while he was wondering about those men and whether they had his mobile yet. And there was Crog too – who was he?

Wilf looked over at him, and then looked again. Why hadn't he noticed? There was a lump under that kaftan. 'What've you got there?' he asked.

Crog clutched the lump with both hands. His eyes were embers.

'What is that?' said Wilf, though already he knew.

'The offering bowl,' replied Crog. 'It bade me come.'

'But I've only just got that!' protested Wilf. 'Why should I give it to you? And who said you could go looking under my bed?'

'What's that?' Ishbel was preparing to go out; she was wearing ankle boots and had swung a small bag over her shoulder. 'What's he got there?'

'A bowl,' said Wilf. '*My* bowl.'

'I failed afore, I must not fail again,' said Crog, still clutching the lump in his kaftan.

'Go on. Show us it, then,' said Ishbel.

Crog looked mistrustfully at Wilf.

'It's all right,' soothed Ishbel. 'He won't touch you.'

He delved down into his kaftan, and slowly – very slowly – brought out the bowl. He held it up to the light.

No one spoke. The rim of gold was very slender, and the bowl itself, Wilf realized, seemed to draw your eye into its curves. Then you could see beyond the surface of the wood into a landscape of whorls and ridges. The three faint growth rings seemed like tiny faraway rivers running in and round and beyond.

Perhaps it was the slight tremble in Crog's hand, but there seemed to be tiny, almost imperceptible ripples moving in the bowl – like the stirrings of dreams across the face of a sleeper. Wilf felt blissfully heavy, as if someone had very lightly pressed fingertips on his eyelids. He awakened with a jolt and found his head had lurched right forward. Feeling foolish, he moved back a little.

But Ishbel had come in close too. 'It's beautiful . . . You can even *feel* it's old, can't you,' she said in a hushed voice.

She reached forward, but Crog drew the bowl back close to his chest. He cradled it with one arm and ran a finger along the gold rim. He no longer looked quite so pinched and peaky. Wilf didn't know whether it was the cornflakes and toast that had filled him out. Or holding the bowl.

'Remember, it's mine,' said Wilf.

Crog ran his finger around the rim again.

'Give it back.'

Crog ignored him.

Wilf made a grab for the bowl. Crog yelped and bent

38

over double, his arms tucked in, protecting the bowl. He stared up at Wilf and repeated, 'I failed afore. I must not fail again.'

Ishbel took hold of Wilf's wrists. 'Let him keep it, Wilf,' she said. 'You don't need it. You only nicked it because you're bored and stupid and enjoy the challenge. You've got everything already.'

'It's mine!'

'It's not yours. Let him have it! If you don't, I'll tell Dad. And I'll tell Mr Robertson, and then you'll have broken the terms of your probation order, and you know what that means!'

Wilf shut his eyes. He couldn't bear that tone of hers.

'That means a custodial sentence, Wilf. Just for once you'll have to pay for what you've done.'

'All right,' snapped Wilf. 'No need to rub it in.'

Ishbel let him go and he rubbed his wrists. After a pause he said, 'There's a slight complication.'

'Go on,' said Ishbel in a heard-it-all-before voice.

'There's someone else quite keen on it . . .'

'And who might that be?'

'Some security guys. Not police, I think,' said Wilf. 'We had this kind of . . . *thing* yesterday. I suppose you'd call it a chase.'

Ishbel gave him a stony look and turned away.

While she made another pot of coffee, Crog disappeared into the utility room, and when he came back the lump under his kaftan was bulkier and had edges. Wilf wasn't in the mood to ask questions – he just sat at the kitchen table and drank his coffee and thought about holding the bowl. The only sound came from Gordon and his exercise ball banging into the walls.

After a while Crog gave a loud, mucus-laden sniff, and said, 'They are with us.'

And then the telephone rang. Only it didn't quite ring; instead the sound was slighter – a tiny electronic cough. Wilf knew that cough.

He ran out onto the balcony, and Ishbel followed him.

He looked first at the front plaza – a large paved area with a few flowerbeds. Nobody there. And nobody at the metal perimeter fence. But the big electronic security gates were wide open. That was unusual.

'They're nearer than you think,' said Ishbel quietly. She was down on her knees, peering directly underneath the balcony.

Wilf looked too. Six storeys below, two men in suits were walking briskly up the steps to the front entrance. It was definitely them – he saw the white stripe of Badger's hair.

'Oh no, Wilf,' said Ishbel. 'Dad'll kill you.'

'It's all right,' he told her. 'Jenkins won't let them through. It's Fort Knox here. They can't just barge in.'

'They can if they have a warrant.'

Crog had come out onto the balcony and was standing behind them, eyes the size of dinner plates. He'd seen the men too.

Wilf said, 'Don't worry, Crog. Security here is dead tight. It's all infrared scanners and bulletproof glass. Nobody can get through the inner doors if Jenkins doesn't press his little button.'

Ishbel nudged him. He looked down again. The men weren't waiting at the top of the steps. Had Jenkins buzzed them in?

Wilf ran back to the hallway and pressed the touchpad for the CCTV screens. His heart thumping, he scanned through the front atrium cameras. The place seemed empty. Where was Jenkins? What was happening?

He flicked on the overhead aerial camera. A dot showed up – something small and dark and reddish against the white marble floor. He zoomed in. In
Suddenly he felt bile rise from his stomach. Isb'
a whimper and covered her eyes. Wilf stopp
had to turn his face away.

The thing on the screen was dark

long bloody tendril dangling down. The thing had once been round and soft, but it had burst – a pale jelly and more blood seeping out of one side where it had been crushed on landing. There was still a small halo of blue. The iris, of course. This had once been an eye.

'Can't be human,' said Wilf.

'Yes it can . . .' Ishbel had flicked through the camera settings. There on the screen was a close-up of the far side of the reception desk. Jenkins was lying flat on his back, hidden behind his chair. A shaft of bone was sticking through where his nose had been mashed. And his other eye was out too, but still hanging from a tendril of optic nerve.

Wilf flicked on the touchpad and panned out. As he did so, he saw the door to the emergency staircase swing shut.

They were coming up.

His thoughts scattered. He could feel his bowels loosening. There must be *something* they could do. Hide here in the flat? But these men – and they certainly weren't police – would find them. Jump from the balcony? They were six floors up. At least there would be that little moment of freedom before the end.

There was a faint pinging noise. A red light was

flashing on the maintenance console by the front door. The lifts were 'out of order'.

'They'll be taking the stairs,' said Wilf. 'Which gives us about four minutes.'

'Does it matter?' said Ishbel. 'There's no other way out now. No way down. We're trapped.'

CHAPTER 5

Wilf felt something tugging at the back of his jacket. It was Crog.

'The hole . . .' he said quietly.

'What?' said Ishbel and Wilf together.

'The hole you threw my gownies down.' Crog pointed to the utility room.

'He means the laundry chute,' said Wilf.

Ishbel was aghast. 'It's just a hole. A huge black hole!'

'Yup.' Wilf dived past them into the utility room. 'But it's a huge black hole with rungs down the side. Now, quick!'

The hatch to the laundry chute was set above a kitchen unit. Wilf pranged the safety catch and held the lid open while Ishbel climbed up onto the work surface, her handbag still over her shoulder. Quickly she lowered herself backwards into the hole.

Crog had found a little rucksack of Ishbel's and was now wriggling the straps onto his shoulders.

'Get in,' said Wilf, hoisting him up onto the worktop. There was almost no weight to him.

Crog crouched on the threshold of the hatch.

'Hurry up!' said Wilf. He gave Crog's bony bum a shove.

Crog scuttled down into the hatch and Wilf clambered in after him. For just a moment before the hatch swung closed, he thought he smelled burning.

The shaft was hot and narrow and dark as a grave. Wilf hated the stale air; he could hear the heavy, sobbing breath of someone – Crog? Or was it Ishbel? – below him.

He gripped the rungs like a sailor clinging to the rigging. If he fell, it was six storeys. No. Seven – for the shaft went down to the laundry in the basement. That was seven storeys to fall, and he'd take the others with him.

He lowered himself down the first few rungs, never releasing more than one foot or hand at any one time. The metal was slippery. He stopped to wipe the slime off his hands and onto his jeans. He climbed down another few rungs, then stopped again and wiped.

He must speed up. The men would look everywhere – at any moment they might open the hatch and shine a torch down. All they had to do then was press the button for the pulley. The lift would come charging up, and then all three of them would be obliterated. Someone would have to scrape their remains off the walls afterwards. Even the organ banks wouldn't be interested.

Wilf tried to go faster but was terrified of losing his grip; he kept having to stop to wipe his hands. Soon his jeans had two great damp patches on the hips. Now he was breathing hard too. Would they be found out? This great throat down the middle of Wilton Towers was an obvious hiding place, if you knew about it. Would the men think to open the hatch? They'd be ransacking the place now. A sudden horrible thought made Wilf's face flush. Gordon! They'd left the hamster in his exercise ball.

Wilf came to a wider gap in the rungs. As he passed his hand across the space, he felt the frame of the rubber seal in the wall. This must be one of the other hatches. The fifth floor? Or the fourth? Maybe they could get out here. He pushed. The door didn't give at all. He pushed again, harder. It still didn't move. This door, and probably all the other hatch doors, could only be opened from *inside* the flats. So there was no way out.

Which would be the worse death? Trapped in an exercise ball? Or in a laundry chute? He clenched his teeth and gave his slippery hands another wipe. He told himself not to dwell on it. The important thing was to keep going.

And he kept going. Climbing on, down and down, and

all the time praying for an exit at the foot of the shaft.

His arms ached; his shoulders felt as though an incubus – something at least the size of Crog – were sitting on them. Surely they must be near the bottom now . . . Surely . . .

But there were more and more rungs.

'You all right?' he whispered. The echo spiralled up and down the length of the shaft, forming a fading chorus of *All rights*.

'All right,' Ishbel whispered back, and again the sound travelled up and down the shaft.

He'd heard nothing from Crog, except little sobs of breath. 'OK, Crog?' he asked.

'Mmm,' replied Crog in a small, high voice.

Wilf wiped his hands again – his trousers were so soggy he had to use his sweatshirt now – and went on down. And down. And down.

The shaft was getting stuffier and hotter. And from somewhere, far off, came a very faint scratch of sound. It was electronic. A car alarm maybe? Wilf's feet slithered on the wet rungs.

Gradually, over the next few metres of descent, he became aware that something was changing. They were approaching the foot of the shaft.

'I'm at the bottom,' said Ishbel.

Wilf stopped and waited. He heard a grunt. Ishbel breathing heavily. 'Push!' he hissed.

'I *am* pushing. It's blocked. Completely blocked. I can't open it.'

'Try the sides,' said Wilf.

'Hold on. There's something here . . . It's a lever!'

Ishbel gave another grunt and a metal flap crashed open. Light spilled into the shaft, blinding them all for a moment. They covered their ears – the fire alarm was blaring. Blue light flashed from the window high up on the laundry wall.

They jumped down onto the floor. There was no one here; just piles of black plastic bags everywhere, and ironed sheets stacked up in plastic crates.

'Let's get out of here!' shouted Wilf. He could hardly think for the blaring of the siren.

'Wait a minute . . .' Ishbel glanced at a row of shoes lined up against one wall. She hovered for a second, and then grabbed a small pair of women's trainers. 'Crog, stand still. You can't go out without shoes.'

Crog lifted his legs one at a time and she jammed the trainers on his feet.

Wilf climbed up onto a dryer, and from the window saw a scene straight from a cop movie: flashing lights, an ambulance, firemen with hoses, and police – *real* police; uniformed, hard-hatted, truncheon-bearing police.

He quickly ducked his head down. 'Let's try the back,' he said.

The basement was a labyrinth of little service rooms. They ran through a post room and down a corridor that led to a little kitchen with a small high window looking out onto the back of the building. Wilf clambered up on a chair and peered out through the security grille. There was Snout standing facing the door. Wilf had another look at him: short grey hair greased back, signet ring, earring, scores of crow's feet around the eyes. He looked hard. Very hard. A real murderer.

Wilf ducked his head down again. 'One of them's standing guard,' he said.

'We'll have to go out the front,' said Ishbel.

'Are you mad? There are police everywhere.'

'That's our only choice,' she told Wilf. 'There's no other way.'

They ran back to the laundry room, and up the stairs. At the ground-floor landing they came upon a throng of residents and all their maids and cleaners and secretaries, and the laundry and gym staff, and the swimming-pool attendants. Everyone was backed up on the st pushing their way towards the lobby and out of the building.

'You can't keep us here! We'll burn to death!' shouted one of the women.

'There's a murderer on the loose!' shouted another. 'We have to get through!'

'All in good time,' said a policewoman firmly. 'Please stop pushing at the back. We are evacuating the building – if everyone stays calm we can all leave safely. The fire is contained. It's only on the sixth floor. You can't all leave at once – we need to give forensics some space.'

Wilf edged his way forward with the crowd; he peered over the shoulder of an elderly man into the lobby. Two men in white jumpsuits and gloves were kneeling down next to Jenkins's body. They had tweezers and were putting things in little plastic bags. Maybe they'd taken Jenkins's eye – what was left of it.

The police had set up another cordon in front of the main entrance. Behind the ribbon there were scores — journalists, television cameramen, some of whom had even set up small

dger? He would be somewhere in for Wilf. They had killed Jenkins.

They could – they *would* – kill again. No doubt about that.

Wilf enjoyed a little bit of fear. It always was an exciting sensation – kept his mind sharp and his fingers tingly. But not this. It felt as if the end of his life was bounding towards him. A bad end too – certain and painful and pointless.

There was nothing he could do. Nowhere he could run to. How could he run anyway? His insides had seized up and cramps were shooting up his legs.

He felt a tap on his shoulder.

Ishbel was behind him and she was holding Crog's hand. 'Can you see them?' she whispered.

'No, but they'll be there.'

'Let's split up. You'll be faster on your own. I'll take Crog,' said Ishbel.

'Meet up at the back of Tesco,' hissed Wilf.

Ishbel shook her head. 'No. Manders's shop.'

Wilf nodded. She was right. Nobody would think to look for them at Manders's.

In the lobby, one of the men in a white jumpsuit covered Jenkins's body with a white sheet. The police-women raised her voice above the chatter of the crowd and called out, 'Please wait your turn in an orderly manner, thank you.'

Everyone was heaving forward, but Wilf hung back.

He had to get himself into the middle of a big group of people. He had to do it fast, for those who'd been at the front were now walking quickly out into the lobby, past the white sheet on the floor and down the front steps. They walked four or five abreast. Would he be hidden? He doubted it.

He waited, holding his nerve. This group and the next group were too thinly spread out. Ishbel and Crog passed him, his sister casting him a warning look. He must join the crowd soon. But nowhere seemed right . . . If he left it too late, he'd be right at the back. Then he could be picked off easily.

He spotted a group of middle-aged women who had been stuck on the stairs together and were now just making their way into the lobby. He sidled up alongside them. He wasn't very tall and some of them had long, sweeping coats. Maybe he could just shuffle along un-noticed in their midst? He ducked round to get nearer the middle of the group.

One of the women gave a little start of surprise. 'Why, Wilfred!' she exclaimed.

It was Mrs Myerson from the third floor. Kindly, and very garrulous. Now all the women were staring at him.

'You don't look at all well!' she went on, unwittingly giving him his cue.

Wilf looked at her soulfully. That woman had so much powder on her face she'd dissolve if you dipped her in water. 'It's my nerves, Mrs Myerson. I'm frightened of the cameras. I really don't want the press to take pictures. My father is very sensitive about publicity.'

'Is he?' Mrs Myerson looked puzzled. 'Well, of course, Wilf. He's an important man.'

'Well, you know . . . and with us not having a mother . . .' he murmured. It was a low blow. But low blows were always the best.

She made a clucking noise. 'You come along with us, dear.'

The people behind were surging forward, and they were half propelled into the lobby. Wilf, in the midst of this phalanx, kept his head down, and the crowd was like a river, pushing him forward. As they passed the body, everyone slowed for a moment, and he glimpsed that white sheet, with a small red stain blooming through the material where Jenkins's head was. But then came another surge, and they were out through the front door into the cold spring air and down the steps, to face the flashing cameras of the press.

Wilf didn't look up, but sideways. Immediately he lowered his head. He was sure he'd seen Badger, with a small spy glass pressed to one eye.

Wilf bobbed back down, praying, *If I don't see him, he won't see me*. He concentrated on getting his legs to work. Right foot in front of left foot. A memory of a biology lesson came into his mind. The teacher had taken a frog, made two little cuts with his scalpel: one at the neck, one at the rump. Then he'd pulled out the spinal cord, terminating the animal. This was called 'pithing' a frog. And now Wilf felt pithed, just like that frog.

The procession of residents moved on. Wilf moved on too – his legs miraculously continuing to propel him forward. They passed the police vans. A policeman with a badge saying VICTIM SUPPORT was ushering them towards a church hall.

When they turned the first corner, Wilf broke free and ran. He didn't look back. He didn't hear his shoes pounding the pavement, or his chest heaving for breath. He barely noticed the shops and the turnings and the traffic lights whirring past. Every tiny filament of his body was ringing with adrenalin. It was so easy. His miserable, scrawny, twenty-a-day, fag-ash body just sprang through the air. How he flew.

CHAPTER 6

Manders was an old rock-'n'-roller with rings on every finger and grey hair down to her waist. Her shop smelled of cats, and she sold old, scratchy vinyls and grungy mementos from the garages of other ageing rock-'n'-rollers. It was a mystery how she ever made any money; nothing cost more than £10 and there were often more people in the back of the shop than the front.

She had seen everything – as had her customers. So when Wilf charged through the door and stood doubled over, gasping for air and holding onto the counter, she didn't look surprised. She just gave a quick jerk of her head to indicate the back room.

Ishbel and Crog were already there, huddled on a sofa by the fire. They looked like bedraggled strays – their faces and clothes dirty, their hair a mess. Wilf realized he must look equally filthy – thanks to the laundry chute. Yet earlier he had barely noticed the dirt.

Neither Ishbel nor Crog looked up at him.

'You've been smoking too many death sticks, Wilf,' murmured Ishbel.

He ignored her.

Some kind person (probably Manders) had put a tea tray down on the table. Ishbel poured, her hands so shaky that the hot liquid slopped everywhere. Wilf took his mug but he couldn't drink. He was still too out of breath – his body didn't seem to realize he wasn't running any more. But Crog downed the tea eagerly, slurping and gurgling like a half-blocked drain.

Eventually it was Ishbel who spoke.

'We could have been killed.' She stared fixedly at the carpet. 'We nearly were.'

Crog nodded.

'Those men, who are they?' she asked.

'Men. Bad men. They wish for the bowl. What they did unto that man . . . that is but the beginning,' said Crog.

'Then let's just give them their bowl back and be done with it,' said Ishbel.

Crog put the rucksack on his knees. He had a peaky, sucked-in look about him.

'It may be a lovely thing, but it's only a bowl,' she went on.

Crog shook his head. From the rucksack he brought out a square wooden box with air holes in the sides.

'Hey!' said Wilf indignantly. 'That's Gordon's. We use it to take him to the vet's.'

'It needs must be covered,' said Crog. 'You had no gold caskets in your house. No helmets.'

'We do! There's my cycling helmet in the hall.'

'Forged of burnished bronze?' asked Crog reproachfully.

'Afraid not,' said Ishbel. 'Even stupidly rich people like us don't run to bronze helmets. It'll be some resin or plastic.'

Crog clicked his tongue disapprovingly. He undid the latch on the box and took out some bits of crumpled aluminium foil. Wilf looked at the foil carefully. Where had that come from? His jacket lining probably. He sighed, envying Crog his quick fingers.

Then Crog delved into the box with both hands and, very carefully, brought out the bowl; and just as he had back in the kitchen, he held it up to the light.

Wilf leaned forward. As his eyes once again traced the faint rings in the wood, he hunkered down into himself and his mind settled. He heard a bird give a rising call, and a tree snared its branches suddenly on the window. But Wilf didn't start: his breathing felt calmer now and, looking at the bowl, he sensed, even in this poky back room, the great world outside revolving under his feet. It was an odd sensation – the little concerns of his life no longer mattered in this lighter, slower time.

He looked over at Ishbel and she gave him a strange, distant smile.

'The bowl is old,' explained Crog. 'Very old. From the time of the great oaks. They were the kings of trees, tall as your high houses here, and strong as mountains. This bowl is made from the heartwood of the last great oak. That was long afore my days and afore my father's days and afore his father's too. In those times the land was alive to us and the rivers ran full and the groves sang and the air was soft and fresh as the green leaves of spring. Then we knew the calls of the wind and the byways of the moon and the thoughts of the water vole.'

When Crog finished his speech, there was a pause as stillness settled on the room.

Eventually Ishbel spoke. 'I didn't know you had so much poetry in you, Crog. At first you barely uttered a squeak and now you're suddenly most eloquent. Who wants more tea?'

But nobody wanted more tea. Wilf, feeling as if he were
ʒ up for air, looked again at the bowl. 'What you
Crog . . . was that *all* animals? Could we have,
ad Gordon? I've always wondered if he
rcise ball.'

'Wilf!' said Ishbel.

'I'm not joking,' he insisted.

'Even your little mouse' – Crog looked sharply at Wilf – 'those men, they kill your mouse. They kill for the pleasure of it.'

Then Ishbel said, 'Crog, I still don't understand. Who are *they*? Who are these men? Where are they from? Don't they have a name?'

'*They. Them*. The valley men. Do not grace them with a name,' said Crog venomously. 'They wish for the bowl.'

'So what's the problem? We just go to the police. Wilf fesses up. We hand over the bowl. We describe those two men. Job done. We've nothing to lose at this point.'

'Oh yes we have,' said Wilf. 'Remember what Mr Robertson said about last-chance saloon.'

'But this is different!' exclaimed Ishbel. 'A man's been murdered!'

'And you think the rozzers won't lay that on me too?' said Wilf. 'They'll nab anyone. And what about those men? They're not going to go away quietly. They've already killed, and we'll be next. Get real, Ishie.'

Crog gave a long hawking sniff and tucked the bowl back into the box. 'When the great trees died and the world turned dry and old, this bowl was all our people had. We forged the gold around the rim and we kept the bowl sacred. We fed it with our souls. With our mead and our honey and our milk. Now it must be safe again. If *they* get it . . .' He shook his head.

'If *they* get it, then *what*?' said Wilf.

Crog shut his eyes and breathed out. His shoulders juddered slightly. 'None will be spared. Not the wain bound in the basket, nor the young maid in the marriage bower, nor the venerable on the shores of death. And with thee' – here Crog looked at Wilf and Ishbel; he snapped his forefinger, making a wet cracking sound – '*they* will do just as they did unto the mouse.'

'*They* don't have to get the bowl,' protested Ishbel. 'We can hide it.'

Crog gave her a pitying look. 'They will always find it. The bowl must go back. This is wherefore I was sent.'

'Go back?' said Wilf. 'So we return it to the museum?'

'Nay!' exclaimed Crog. 'For there the valley men will take it!'

'Couldn't you just throw it in the Thames, then?' asked Ishbel.

Crog looked blank.

'The river. Here,' she explained.

Crog stared at her, aghast.

'Well, *where*, then?' said Wilf.

60

'I failed afore. I must not fail again,' intoned Crog.

'I wish you wouldn't keep saying that. Back where? Where does the bowl need to go?'

Crog swayed slightly in his seat, a crease of concentration appearing between his eyebrows. He paused, and Wilf looked at him again and thought, *His head is really far too big for that little stalk of a neck. At least the rope balances things out a bit.*

Finally Crog said, 'A place of joining between this world and the next. I know but one. Where the mountains rise to the sky and the wild dogs roar and the sea and the sweet water meet.'

'Wild dogs?' asked Wilf. 'What wild dogs?'

Ishbel added, 'Crog, we don't have wild dogs nowadays. There's no rabies in Britain, I'm glad to say.'

'Wild dogs *of the sea*,' corrected Crog. 'The water rises and spits like as to a pack of wild dogs.'

'Oh, I see. You're just talking about waves, breaking waves. I wish you'd be a bit clearer. But where is this place?'

'That way.' Crog pointed out of the window. 'Towards the mountains.'

'Wait a minute . . . I've not used this app before.' Ishbel clicked on the compass on her phone. 'North?' she asked.

Crog nodded.

Manders had been in the back kitchen. Now she came in carrying a plastic basin of hot soapy water. Over one arm she had some scraps of material and a hand towel.

'You can clean yourself up, kids. Use the rags as flannels,' she said, placing the basin on the coffee table.

Ishbel immediately took up a rag and swiftly wiped herself clean. Wilf and Crog were slower. They were still tentatively dipping their rags into the water when Ishbel was drying herself off on the towel. She started rubbing at the grimy patches on her hoodie.

When Manders returned to the front of the shop, Wilf said, 'She never asks questions. That's the great thing about her.'

'It's only sensible, isn't it?' said Ishbel. 'What you never know, you never have to deny.'

She turned her head to make sure that Manders was truly out of earshot. Then she spoke quietly, steepling her varnished fingernails to form a little red roof. 'Where were we . . . ? So, we know that Crog's place is somewhere north with mountains. That's a bit vague. It could mean the Lake District. Or Scotland. And what's north of Scotland? Blimey – it could mean Iceland. And how exactly do you propose getting there?'

Crog looked at her, bemused. 'With my legs.'

'You can't walk!' said Wilf. 'It's four hundred miles to Scotland.'

'And if it's Iceland, you might find walking there pretty tough too,' added Ishbel with a smirk.

'But I have no oxen, nor no mule, nor no—' Crog stopped. A little uncertainly he added, 'Nor no journeying box.'

'We don't have a car,' said Ishbel flatly. She looked at Wilf. 'He can't fly. He doesn't have any documents. Rail's his best bet.'

'*Our* best bet. Come on, Ishie! We have to go with him,' said Wilf. What impulse had made him say that? He didn't know. He certainly needed to keep the bowl close. And maybe – he was less sure about this – he wanted to be near strange little Crog as well. And at least the journey would be a bit different; a bit scary too. It certainly wouldn't be boring.

'No we don't,' she retorted. 'We don't have to do anything.'

'We do,' said Wilf. 'He can't go alone. He won't even know what a *train* is. He wouldn't survive a minute on his own.'

'Speak for yourself. You can go. *I* don't have to. And how come one minute you're stealing that bowl and the next you are dead set on returning it? You're just creating work for yourself. It doesn't make sense.'

'Come on!' pleaded Wilf.

'I told you. I'm not coming.'

'Why not? Somebody's got to look after him! And you can't go home!' said Wilf.

Ishbel's voice was cold and clipped. 'No, I can't go home, can I? Not when those men – those *murderers* – know where we live.' She looked at him scornfully. 'But you didn't think of that, did you, buster? It's what Mr Robertson always says, isn't it? *You never think of the consequences.* You always rely on Dad to bail you out. And it won't work this time.'

'Not now, Ishie,' said Wilf. 'Leave Mr Robertson out of this. We're all in this together.'

'Thanks to you.'

'Oh, *please!*'

'I said I'm not going. Why should I? I didn't steal the bowl.'

'So where'll you go, then?' said Wilf.

'I'll go to Melissa's. Or Carol's – she's not going away this half term. Carol's mum says that I bring out the best in her. She says, *Ishbel, you're a real ray of sunshine.*'

'You won't be a real ray of sunshine when those men smash down her front door,' Wilf pointed out.

'Leave me alone!' cried Ishbel.

'How can I? You're in on this, whether you like it or not. You're in up to your eyeballs.'

Ishbel looked up at the corner of the ceiling and pursed her lips.

'Sorr-ee!' said Wilf. 'I shouldn't mention eyes now, should I? But I think we should try Scotland first.'

'Scotland!' Ishbel grimaced.

'Yeah! Scotland. Home of our forefathers. Mum's resting place. Where we really ought to be.'

'Scotland' – Ishbel pulled herself together – 'is wet and cold and full of midges. And the mobile reception is rubbish.'

'That's 'cos there are real mountains there. And, Ishie, we haven't been for years.'

'Nope,' she said. 'And we should take the train.'

So she *was* going to come. Wilf smiled at her.

Ishbel jiggled Crog's arm, put on her for-foreigners voice and said slowly, 'A train is a very big, very long sort of journeying box. And there are only two roads north for the trains. One up the west coast of England and one up the east coast.'

Crog nodded. 'Yes. Hills . . . The land has a spine like a beast.'

Just for a moment Ishbel looked appraisingly at Crog.

Then she went on, 'So this place you want to go to . . . Can you see it in your mind?'

'I know it,' replied Crog.

'And on which side of the land is the sea?'

Crog pointed west.

Ishbel thought for a moment. 'OK,' she said, smiling with satisfaction. 'If the sea is facing that way, our mystery location must be on the west coast. So we'll take the west coast line to Glasgow. And' – she tapped something into her mobile and waited for a moment – 'that means Euston Station.'

Manders returned. This time she was carrying a bundle of clothes so high that her eyes were only just visible over the top. Ishbel and Wilf stood up and helped her to set down the tottering bundle.

'If you happen to be going up north,' said Manders tactfully, 'you'll need proper coats.'

With that, she left them.

The clothes were from the shop's second-hand clothes rail and most were party outfits – with crusted old brocade and moulting velvet. Ishbel and Wilf, who liked nothing better than dressing up, fell on the pile. Halfway down the pile Wilf saw a glint of silver and pulled out a studded leather jacket. It smelled doggy and the arms were a bit long, but once he'd rolled the cuffs up it was comfortable.

Ishbel picked out a long black cloak. She hooked it on and twirled around. Crog, who was making no attempt to find anything for himself, looked impressed. But Wilf said, 'That's hopeless. You can't run in a cloak. You're not a wizard in Harry Potter.'

Then she picked out a padded satin jacket in lilac.

'I suppose you never think about clothes being useful?' said Wilf.

'No, not really,' she replied, stroking the satin. 'Nice, isn't it? It's Italian.'

'They'll spot you a mile off,' said Wilf. 'And when they do get you, the colour will clash with your blood stains.'

Ishbel gave him a cold look. Instead she put on a dark green oilskin.

They had, Wilf was sure, been wasting time – the clothes had distracted them. How could they be so foolish!

He turned to Crog. 'Where do you think those men are?'

Crog shrugged unhappily.

'So they could be on our trail right now?'

'They are fleet of foot,' said Crog. 'We will not be safe now. Never.'

'That's nice to know,' replied Wilf. 'And there's no point waiting for them to catch up with us here, is there?'

He got to his feet quickly, steadying himself on the arm of the sofa, and went to the window. Out the back of Manders's shop was a small mossy patio, which was surrounded – as Wilf knew from previous experiences – by wobbly fencing that led to other small mossy patios in every direction. Fine for slugs, but not for people.

Better check out the front.

Wilf walked into the shop, and flattened himself against the side wall. As he sidled up to the window, Manders flashed him a knowing smile.

He strained his ears but couldn't hear anything; just a background blur of city noises. He looked out quickly – the street really did seem empty. He checked along the parked cars. No silver Mercedes. Nobody waiting for them.

Not yet.

Wilf checked the street once more. It wasn't far to Wapping Station. And once they had made it onto the Jubilee Line, they'd be underground. And maybe being underground would help protect them.

He ran through the shop. In the back room Ishbel had been searching through the clothes. Crog was now wearing a bobble hat and a scarf which at least covered part of his face and that terrible rope.

Manders saw them off. She shook hands with Crog,

and embraced Ishbel. She ruffled Wilf's hair and he gave her what Ishbel called his 'sentence skipper' – the intensely endearing grin that had liquefied the resolve of so many magistrates.

Manders hugged him all the tighter. 'Get going,' she said. 'Look after yourselves. And your little cousin.'

Wilf rubbed the gooseflesh on his arms. As he opened the shop door, he heard that birdsong again.

CHAPTER 7

They queued up at the ticket counter and Ishbel bought three children's return fares to Glasgow. Crog watched her.

'Tickets,' she said as she put the tickets in her wallet.

'Tickets?' said Crog.

'They allow us to get on the train,' she told him. 'Come on, where've you been? Do I have to explain *everything* to you?'

'No,' he replied stiffly. 'These ways are new to me, but I know the old lore.'

It was forty minutes till the next Glasgow train left, so they sat in a café up on the balcony of the station atrium. It was a good vantage point – there was a bank of security cameras and they could see everyone coming and going in the hall below.

Ishbel picked up a menu. Crog did the same, pressing it against his face and sniffing at the plastic coating.

There was a little rack of condiments on the table. Wilf dreamily poured out a little mountain of salt and another of sugar and mixed them together with his fore-finger.

'Do you have to do that?' said Ishbel.

'Er, no . . .' Wilf gave her a big sleepy smile. 'But look – it's our little place of joining . . . where the sweet and the salt crystals meet.'

Ishbel rolled her eyes. 'Listen, Crog,' she said. 'Here's the choice. Do you want meat?'

Crog nodded vigorously.

'Thought you would . . . And with it you can have some long finger-shaped bits of root that have been cooked in grease. Or a big round root that has been in the oven and had things put inside it. If I were you, I'd go for the fingers.'

'Fingers,' said Crog.

'Fingers *what*,' pressed Ishbel.

'Fingers *please*.'

'Ishie!' said Wilf.

'Well, I'm paying for them!' Ishbel turned to him. 'I don't suppose you brought a wallet with you, did you? You're like royalty – above such things as money. No, I take that back. You just nick everything instead.'

'Fingers *please*,' said Crog quietly.

'Fingers *please*,' repeated Crog, less quietly this time.

Ishbel ordered steak and chips and Coke for everyone.

She asked for the bill immediately and handed the waiter her debit card. She didn't look like she wanted to be asked any questions, but that didn't stop Crog.

'The thing . . .' He nodded at her debit card. 'The thing is master?'

'Well done, Crog!' she exclaimed. 'Yes, it's like a MasterCard.'

'That's not what he means,' muttered Wilf.

'Master,' repeated Crog. 'It is master. Not the bearer. It rules. He who has the card makes others his slaves. That is how it is with the bowl.'

When the waitress put down the Coke, Crog picked up his can and brought it to his lips. The space between his eyebrows puckered. He tried the can again.

'You undo it first,' said Wilf. He demonstrated, pulling the tag on his own can. Crog followed suit and a fountain of Coke spilled out onto the table. Ishbel looked away.

When the plates arrived, Crog launched immediately into his steak. Ishbel wouldn't let him pick it up whole. She cut the meat into strips, which he ate fast, chewing noisily. Then he embarked on his chips. He *loved* the chips – and the ketchup, making a big red pool of it on his plate. He loved the brown sauce and made a big pool of that too. He dipped every chip first in the ketchup, then in the brown sauce, then in Wilf's salt-sugar mix. Sometimes he accidentally dipped the end of his rope in too.

When he finished, Ishbel said, 'Skoosh, skoosh?'

Crog nodded.

'Go down the stairs and follow the signs with a man drawn on them. Wash your face while you're there.'

Could he make it on his own? Wilf looked out over the balcony and watched Crog bobbing his way across the station concourse. What on earth was the matter with him? When normal people crossed a crowded space, they just seem to make room for each other effortlessly. But not Crog. He was trying too hard. He went at a crouchy half-walk, half-run, skipping and dodging and darting, and yet forever bumping into people or making them jolt to a sudden stop. How could something so easy be so hard?

'I do wish he'd get rid of that rope,' said Wilf.

'I know,' Ishbel agreed. 'It gives me the creeps. And have you noticed his neck? The skin's all creased and twisted.'

Wilf thought, *His neck has been wrung like a turkey's*. But he said nothing.

'A skin toner might help,' mused Ishbel, smiling slightly. 'How do you think he got like that?'

'No idea. Everything has happened so fast I haven't had time to think.'

'And who is he really?' she asked. 'Where's he from? Is he having us on?'

'It doesn't feel like that, does it? I'm sure he really hasn't used a toilet before, or eaten chips. And those men – they're real enough. Look what happened to Jenkins.'

'Don't.' Ishbel covered her eyes with the heels of her hands and rubbed. 'You know something? Crog may seem as meek as a lamb—'

'But the men aren't,' said Wilf.

'Let me finish. Crog's all quiet and vulnerable and needing help, but he's just turned our lives upside down. Now we're on our way to some godforsaken mountain, and we don't know where, and we don't know why. Yet we're just going along with it all, aren't we?'

'But that's true of life, isn't it?' Wilf pointed out. 'We're always just *going along* with it.'

'No,' said Ishbel. 'I have plans. I have a cello exam next week. Well, I *had* a cello exam next week. And one day I want to be a doctor.'

Wilf took a deep breath. Not for the first time, he considered himself a saint for not slapping her. He turned away and, as he did so, his eye was caught by one of the security screens, which was showing a bizarre little comedy. Two smartly dressed women, one of them holding a wildly wriggling small dog, were watching a suitcase magically lift itself onto their trolley. Wilf looked down into the hall to get the real-life version: the same two flustered-looking women were standing over Crog as he lifted the suitcase up.

Wilf flicked his eyes back to the screen. No Crog. Above the hubbub of the station, he thought he heard the dog squeal.

He looked down again at the hall, just to make sure. There was Crog again, nodding apologetically to the women.

The camera did not see Crog.

Here was something that Wilf had no grasp of, something dangerous. He recalled the chase with Snout and Badger, and how, when he had looked in the reflective glass, the silver Mercedes had seemed to be driving itself. He also remembered Jenkins – how the blood had started to bloom red through the sheet that the police had put over his head.

Wilf hunched his shoulders in fear and felt the sweat creep down his backbone, a little river between two hills. He shut his eyes and tried to think clearly. But the full strangeness of what had happened in the last twenty-four hours washed through him, blurring his mind. How had they ended up here? How had Crog come to be in their flat? How had the three of them just abandoned everything and set off? And what would Dad – if he ever noticed – think? And Mr Robertson? They hadn't had time for a note or anything.

Ishbel must have sensed his terror. She put down her mobile. 'Wilf? What's up?'

'Look!'

She glanced down at the hall. 'Crog's tripped over a trolley? That was predictable . . .'

Wilf pointed to the camera screen. 'Don't you see?'

Ishbel shrugged.

'*No!* Look again! *Crog doesn't show up on the screens!* He doesn't show up! He's *invisible*.'

Ishbel did exactly what Wilf had done. She looked up at the screen, then back down at the concourse, then up at the screen again. There was a long pause. She swallowed hard. 'Wee-erd. That's not possible . . . I don't understand. This "Crog" – this *creature* . . . We don't know where he's from, do we? Is he visible in mirrors? Does he have a reflection? Does he have a shadow?'

'Oi! He's not a vampire!' said Wilf. He remembered Crog and the mirror in the bathroom. Then he decided not to remember it.

'How d'you know? He asked for blood this morning, didn't he?' said Ishbel.

'There isn't an explanation for everything in life. Maybe . . . maybe his electromagnetic waves are a bit strange. I dunno . . .' Wilf trailed off. The mirror in the bathroom had bounced back into his mind again. Crog hadn't been crouching *that* low. He'd just not shown up.

'Or maybe . . .' pressed Ishbel. 'Maybe he really *does* come from another world?'

'Sometimes I think *you've* come from another world,' said Wilf.

'Try and be serious for once. Think it through, Wilf. Here he is, defying the laws of physics. And he's never seen a bathroom. Or a fridge. And the way he talks . . .'

'It's just a quirk,' said Wilf. Why did Ishie always have to think everything through to the bitter end?

'*And* we've never worked out how he got into the flat,' she added.

'There must be another explanation for all this,' said Wilf. 'It's just we haven't thought of it.'

'No. You don't get it, do you?' Ishbel was suddenly certain. 'He *must* have come from another world. The question is, what or who has he brought with him?'

'Something happened yesterday which I didn't

tell you about,' said Wilf. 'You know those two men . . .?'

Ishbel nodded.

'They don't show up in mirrors, either.'

'Which means that everything in our lives – every truth and every person we hold dear – is now up for grabs.'

Wilf looked across the table at his twin. She was – as always – neatly dressed: the oilskin suited her and her hair hung in a neat glossy curtain down over her shoulders. But her face was deathly pale.

'Let's get out of here!' he said.

CHAPTER 8

They had a table to themselves. Ishbel sat straight-backed and watchful. When the train began to move, she exhaled loudly and slumped back in her seat, eyes glazed. Her mobile was held limply in one hand.

Wilf watched the aisle in both directions. 'No sign of *them*,' he said quietly.

The grubby backside of north London began to whirr past – greasy grass sidings, rubbish heaps, gardens full of broken tricycles and cars on bricks. Crog sat with the rucksack on his lap and his nose pressed against the glass, staring – was it *through* or just *at* the glass? Wilf couldn't tell. It was like a dog watching telly: you never knew.

'Crog, let me get this straight,' said Ishbel. 'Those two men . . . are they like you? Are they from the past – are they kind of ghosts?'

Crog fiddled with the ends of his rope. 'They are of the valley people. Once they too were cast into darkness, but now they are with us, of this world. And should we rest, they will fall upon us like wolves.'

Wilf turned to him. 'So if they're like you, how come they aren't in funny brown clothes?'

'Yeah,' said Ishbel. 'And how come they've got mobiles and you don't even know what a toilet is?'

Crog looked disdainful. 'The valley people were laden with gold. Their bowls were full, their cattle fat, their arrows fletched with the finest hawk feathers. When they come now, it is the same. They have all things. The best of women, the best of weapons.'

'And accessories too,' added Ishbel. 'Did you get a load of their shoes? They've been off down Bond Street. One of them was wearing ostrich-skin loafers.'

'Ostrich! That's what it was,' said Wilf. 'But how do you know that, Ishie? You barely saw them! We were six storeys up.'

'You know me,' she said. 'I always notice what people are wearing. Always. Like a dentist notices everyone's teeth. I miss nothing. I can spot a Prada bag at five hundred metres.'

Crog looked down at his bag – the rucksack in his lap – and a small smile appeared on his lips. 'The valley people may have shoes of the finest leather, but that counts for naught against the bowl.'

'Take it out now. Let's have a look at it,' said Wilf. He

wanted to hold the bowl, to feel again that world outside, that wide sky soaring overhead.

But Crog shook his head.

'Why not? Go on. Are you scared I'll take it?'

But Crog gripped the rucksack even more tightly and turned back to the window.

'Can't you be sensitive for once, Wilf?' said Ishbel. 'He doesn't want everyone staring at it.'

Wilf looked down the corridor. It would be good to have a cigarette, but he needed cash for that. A man a few seats down had left his coat hanging over the back of his seat and there was a nice bulge of wallet. How careless. Anyone could just skim past on the way to the toilet – he didn't deserve to keep his cash.

So, should he just lift the wad as it was? Or wait till a passenger was walking this way and form a momentary wallet-relieving jam just by the jacket? Wilf was still weighing up his options when he felt Crog's eyes upon him; Crog looking at him looking at the wallet. Wilf gave him an enormous grin. Crog turned back to the window, but Wilf felt uncomfortable. He'd been put off his stride.

The train trundled on alongside a motorway. The fields of the Midlands were opening up before them: fences, pylons, cows . . . No men, thank God, in ostrich loafers.

As for the cows, Wilf hadn't seen a proper black-and-white cow for a while. Normally they went abroad for their holidays, and there were no cows on Mustique, or in the French ski resorts. Or on the island of Capri. Watching these cows grazing in their fields made him feel calmer.

The man with the wallet got off at Crewe. The platform was all but empty – no sign here of *them*.

The train continued north. Ishbel clicked away on her mobile and Crog, still clutching his rucksack, slumped into a dribbly sleep. Wilf eased back in his seat and watched the endless rise and fall of the hills. Not so many cows now; more sheep. And more colours too: not just the kids'-colouring-book blues and greens of southern England, but more muddled shades – mousy brown hills with last year's bracken and yellow grass, and just an undertow of bile green where the spring shoots were pushing through.

Finally, as they came into Carlisle Station, Crog woke up with a jolt. He pressed his face against the window, eyes flitting from side to side. This time there could be no doubt: he was looking *out* of the window.

'What's the matter, Crog?' asked Ishbel.

He gave one of his long hawking sniffs. '*Them*. They are with us.'

The train came to a stop. They scanned the platform – but all Wilf could see was the usual muddle of passengers getting on and off the train. No sign of *them*.

Not yet.

The engine was making its heaving, ready-to-go noises, and the guard was strolling down the platform, banging the doors closed. He wasn't hurrying, and that meant there was time for a silver Mercedes to skid to a halt in the station car park.

There was a tall metal fence between the car park and the platform. Through the wire mesh they could all see Badger and Snout getting out of the car.

Even though he was accustomed to breaking rules, Wilf assumed that it took a while to get onto a train. You had to go through the entrance and get your ticket, and check (or jump) through the barriers. But not this time. The men weren't going into the station – they were running directly towards the train. Badger reached the fence first, his hand clutching some small object. He drew that same hand very fast down the fence, somehow un-zipping the mesh. It flopped back on either side, and the men burst through and sprinted onto the platform. The porter was closing the last of the doors as they jumped into a carriage at the rear of the train.

The passengers who had just got on were still blocking the corridors, sorting their bags and coats. Muttering excuses, Wilf barged his way forward, and Crog and Ishbel stumbled behind in his slipstream. Through the buffet – nowhere to hide there. In the first-class compartment they had a clear run. Wilf tried to think: where could they go? The roof? But that was all electric cables. The toilets? Lame. Lame. Lame. If Badger could slice open fencing, he'd be through a little door like that in no time.

They reached the front of the train. That was it. Just the locked door to the driver's compartment. And the toilet.

And death.

There was nothing for it. Wilf pressed the OPEN button and the electronic toilet door slid open and they piled in. With excruciating slowness, the door eased itself closed.

Crog crouched on the seat, huddled over his rucksack as if his little scrap of a body could protect the bowl. He was quivering.

Ishbel held her finger against the LOCK button. 'I'll keep holding it,' she said, panting. 'They'll probably try and override the lock electronically; this might just delay them a bit. Wilf, get that window open.'

He cast his eyes around the tiny room. The window was a sealed unit of smoked glass. What could he use? A little red escape hammer was mounted in a case by the sink. Wilf smashed the glass with his fist, and grabbed the hammer in both hands. It felt too light. Using all his body weight, every ounce, he swung it against the window.

There was a useless clunk and the hammer bounced out of his hands. As it landed, the metal tip sheered away from the handle.

Wilf cursed the train, the hammer, and their bad luck. They might as well be dead already.

Crog gave a grunt. He was standing on the toilet seat and he had found an equipment cupboard near the ceiling. With one hand he was holding open a metal flap; with the other he reached in.

'Take hold,' he said, handing down a large metal jack. Wilf grabbed it. The jack felt heavy – this was a proper tool.

'Hurry!' said Ishbel.

Wilf swung the jack at the window. As he did so, he remembered Jenkins, and the thought of that poor man's mangled face gave force to his blow.

This time he hit home. He staggered backwards as a blast of air and broken glass shot into the train. The hole was the size of a football and cold wind poured through it. Holding the jack with both hands, he struck again and again, and the glass disintegrated. Crog helped pull out the remaining pieces.

'You go first!' Wilf had to shout over the wind and the roar of the engine. He could see nothing outside but the green blur of railway sidings. At this speed they'd be dead when they hit the ground.

Then he thought: *The emergency cord!*

Wilf tugged the red handle, and immediately the brakes screeched and the train lurched and slowed as if a gigantic force were pulling at its tail. A scorched smell filled the air.

Crog was up on the windowsill now, hair over his face, one arm nursing the rucksack, ready to fall. The train was still moving fast.

'Do you want me to push?' asked Wilf.

Crog nodded.

So Wilf pushed and Crog fell, with a horrible squeal that was swallowed up by the noise of the train and the wind.

It'll be a quick end, thought Wilf. *At least I pushed him outwards and his body will be out the way of the wheels.*

Ishbel took her finger off the LOCK button and the toilet door juddered slightly, as if it wanted to open.

The lock was making a whirring noise. *They* were there.

'Come on!' said Wilf. As the train slowed, he helped Ishbel onto the windowsill. He couldn't bear to look at her face. He didn't wait to ask. He just shoved her in the back and climbed onto the window ledge after her.

The door was cracking open as he jumped.

CHAPTER 9

It was a brutal landing. Wilf tried to curl into a ball as he fell, but his feet slammed so hard into the embankment that his knees bounced up, smashing into his jaw and making his head whip back. He could hear the scream of brakes – though it was nothing compared to the pain searing through his head.

Gasping, he looked back. Ishbel was coming towards him, hobbling slightly. And further down the track, a little figure was leaning over like a winded athlete. It was Crog! Somehow he too had survived the fall.

Wilf stumbled to his feet. His legs felt OK-ish, but not great. Ahead, just a few metres further down the track, he could see a bridge over a river, where the train was slowing to a halt. It was lucky Wilf had jumped when he did – a few seconds more and he'd have hit the bridge railings. It was lucky too that the river was there: no one could follow him out of that window. But *they* would be out very soon, and running back down those tracks.

Now Ishbel was by his side, and Crog half ran, half

staggered towards them, the rucksack under his arm, his horrible rope bouncing.

'You all right?' asked Ishbel.

Crog gave her a brave, watery smile.

'Come on, then,' said Wilf.

They clambered up the side of the cutting, climbed over some metal railings and came out by a road. On the far side was a housing estate.

Wilf grabbed Crog's hand, amazed to find that his legs still worked. Wheels – that was what they needed. They ran on past some neat little houses. There was no shop, no pub, no cigarette-vending machine. And no people. They passed a couple of new Fords fitted with immobil-izers. Wilf didn't even consider trying them – mean, cheap little cars always had the tightest security systems. Ahh! They came to what Wilf knew was a proper car – a Saab 9.5 estate: three-litre engine, leather upholstery. It would have some speed, and style.

Wilf gave the bumper a quick kick. No alarm. That was good. And Ishbel would have something in her bag.

'I don't like this,' she said, handing him the metal comb from her back pocket.

Wilf pushed it down the gap between the Saab's window and the bodywork. He shut his eyes – somehow it was always easier if you weren't looking – and he wiggled the comb about till it latched onto the mechanism and released the door catch.

The men would be over the bridge and climbing that bank, Wilf thought as he opened the door and got in. Crog stood on the pavement staring at the car. 'Hurry up,' hissed Ishbel, and pushed him into the back seat.

Wilf quickly removed the steering wheel undercasing, pulled out two red wires, tugged off the rubber insulation with his teeth and twisted the wires together. He revved the engine and the car gave a fruity cough. He drove off, swerving out of the housing estate and speeding away from the bridge and the river.

The road bent and dipped into the hills. Wilf was skidding round corners and grinding the gears. He loved driving fast, but not *this* fast. He was checking the rear-view mirror constantly, but there was no sign of the men.

Ishbel sat in the passenger seat, both hands braced on the dashboard to stop herself lurching forward.

Wilf kept his eyes fixed on the road ahead. He'd have to drive fast to escape *them* – if the men had driven that Mercedes from London to Carlisle in time to catch up with an InterCity train, then they must have broken the speed limit the entire way. Or flown? Or apparated? Or . . .

He didn't want to think any more, and instead just

pressed his foot down on the accelerator. There was something hypnotic about driving very, very fast. Tarmac and fence posts whirred past. He reached that tipping point where he was going so fast that he was no longer properly in control of the car. Then he put on yet another spurt of speed.

The corner came towards him so fast that he veered into the middle of the road to manage the turn. A car coming in the opposite direction swerved and blared its horn. Wilf slowed down and checked again in the mirror; still no sign of *them*.

He came to a junction with a sign off to the right – M6, GLASGOW. But he knew that in a 'borrowed' car you were always better off on B roads, where there were fewer traffic patrols. He continued straight on.

The road was now heading northeast, up into the hills, past farmhouses and a few lonely pubs and churches. He'd never been here before, but somehow he seemed to know where he was going. Ishbel had called up the map on her mobile and was following the route, but it felt as if the road were showing them the way, drawing them steadily upwards as the land slanted away below them.

Eventually they came out onto a pass where swathes of mist lay over the fields; the sheep looked as if they were floating.

Wilf stopped at a tiny petrol station – just a shack, with the windows covered in peeling stickers, and piles of old tyres and oil drums everywhere. A tiny oily old man who looked as if he'd spent his life burrowing under cars came out. His hands looked a bit like Crog's.

The little old man was filling up the tank when a lorry coming in the opposite direction swerved into the garage. Wilf gave a start – was it *them*? And then he saw the small paunchy driver and the bags of cement in the back of the lorry.

Still, Wilf thought it better to lie low. While Ishbel went to pay, he stayed in the car – he didn't want to open the door and let anyone see the broken casing and loose wires.

They were just about to set off again when a little electronic cough came from Ishbel's lap. It was a cough he knew well.

'Your mobile! They're on to us!' he hissed.

'What do you mean?' said Ishbel.

'Don't you see? They've been tracking us. How else would they know we were going north. How else would they know we were at Carlisle?'

'But I had the phone on in the train and we never heard anything then,' said Ishbel.

'But there was a lot of other noise going on, wasn't there?' said Wilf.

'I don't understand . . . Are they really tracking us? If so, *how*? Does Crog have some funny tag thing?'

'The card. The mastering card?' said Crog from the back, but Wilf and Ishbel ignored him.

'I dunno, Ishie,' said Wilf, 'but my phone was making that noise too. And so was the landline in the flat.'

'But how would they tag *me*?' asked Ishbel.

Wilf groaned. He was losing patience. 'We've got the same surname. Same address. Same service provider. What do you want, blood? And does it matter *how*? *Just throw it out!*'

A grubby hand reached over from the back seat and grabbed the mobile. Ishbel gave a yelp, but before she could get it back, Crog had run out of the car.

The little old man and the lorry driver were chatting by the pump. They didn't see Crog scuttle round the back of the lorry and throw the mobile in among the cement bags.

'Look, he's setting up a decoy. He's not stupid old Crogsie,' exclaimed Wilf.

'No, he's not,' said Ishbel flatly, 'and that does seem to have taken you for ever to work out.'

They set off again, Wilf looking repeatedly in the rear-view mirror, but there was no car following. And the cement lorry had headed south. So, nothing – just more bare hills, and the dark line of the road spooling out before and behind them.

Ishbel found a road map in the glove pocket and they crossed the border into Scotland. Wilf had slowed down a bit now – he was too tired to risk his life at every turn. The land was gentler now. More fields. More sheep again. Even a few cows. And nothing following.

Wilf thought of the bowl. He still wanted to hold it and feel that sense of mystery and wonder and delight. He angled the rear-view mirror down to see the back seat. Crog was sitting with his knees scrunched up, the rucksack on his lap.

'Crog, are we going in the right direction?' asked Wilf.

Crog smiled. Wilf assumed that meant 'Yes'.

'And are we anywhere near that place?'

Crog shook his head.

'So we're in the backside of nowhere. Where are we going? Can't you say something?'

Crog remained silent.

'So we just go on and on and on?'

Crog smiled again.

And the road did just go on and on and on. Up and down, on and on. More fields. More sheep. Eventually

Wilf said, 'I've had enough now. I'm tired. I could murder a Coke.'

He lifted his gaze from the road. Dusk was coming, and a clammy damp was settling over the fields, making the tarmac shine. The grass was grey, the sky a dark bluey grey. And the sheep were grey – they looked like they could murder a Coke too.

Wilf jostled Ishbel, who had dozed off. 'Why don't we call it a day? Let's find a place for the night.'

'*Where?*' said Ishbel. 'Here? Anyone could spot us a mile off! Let's go somewhere we can hide. Somewhere, you know, really wild.'

'Where? The Cairngorms?'

'No,' said Ishbel. 'Glasgow.'

CHAPTER 10

They never got to Glasgow. Wilf followed signs for the city, and they were just coming into an urban hinterland, when the road suddenly turned into a dual carriageway and threatened to become a motorway. And that, of course, would mean lights and police cameras. So Wilf took the first exit; it led them past scrubland and into a maze of light industrial units and DIY outlets that were already shut down for the night.

Ahead he saw a line of green and white flags. A new housing development. If the flags were up, that meant they were still selling the houses. If they were still selling, there would be a furnished show home to attract the buyers.

He gave the steering wheel a punch.

'What are you so pleased about?' asked Ishbel.

'I've found us a place for the night.'

The lock to the show-home door was a feeble three-pin latch. Wilf opened it in seconds and they walked into a clean, carpeted world that smelled like the inside of a new car. There were artificial orchids everywhere – even in the shower cubicles.

Crog stood completely still in the hallway. He had taken the box out of the rucksack and was holding it against his chest. 'Where are the people?' He spoke in a cracked whisper.

'What people?' said Wilf.

'The people of the house. Are they dead? Out hunting?'

'Nobody lives here,' Ishbel told him. 'It's just a *show* home. To *show* people what it would be like to live here.'

Crog cast his eyes suspiciously around the cream walls.

'Never mind,' said Ishbel. 'You'll feel better after you've freshened up.'

He looked at her stonily.

The show home didn't have any soap, or towels. So they showered using washing-up liquid and dried themselves on the curtains. They didn't dare turn the lights on. But the gas was connected and they lit the fake coal fire in the sitting room.

Wilf put on the kettle. There was nothing to eat in the show house, but Ishbel had found some toffees in the car, and in the master bedroom there was a tray with a bottle of champagne and two fluted glasses.

They drew the curtains and made a nest of cushions and bedcovers on the floor by the fire. The champagne made Wilf feel slightly giddy. Now at last he could relax; it was cosy here – even if the fire gave off little warmth.

But Crog sat bolt upright, both hands round his box.

'What's up with you?' Wilf gave him a prod. 'You've got a face like a slapped bum.'

Crog tightened his grip on the box. 'A fire but not a fire,' he said sourly.

'Well, I suppose that's true,' agreed Ishbel. 'It's not a real fire. It's a real-*effect* fire.'

Crog didn't look up. 'Flowers but not flowers. A home but not a home.'

'Yeah. But the champagne's OK, isn't it?' said Wilf.

'Drink but not drink. Air,' muttered Crog.

'So now you're complaining about the bubbles in the champagne?' said Wilf.

A glimmer of a smile crossed Crog's face. But still he held the box tightly.

'Why don't you put that down?'

Crog shook his head. 'We must hold fast. We must not break the bowl. We must return it to a place of joining. If not, all is over. We become men with no shadows.'

'*Men with no shadows* – what on earth d'you mean?'

'And what about women?' added Ishbel.

'Look where we sit,' said Crog, ignoring Ishbel. 'This

house is not a home. The fire is not a fire. We will become like that – men who are not men.'

'I suppose that means we'll be *real-effect people*,' said Ishbel with a little laugh.

But Crog nodded.

'More champagne?' asked Wilf.

Crog nodded again.

Later, when Crog and Ishbel had settled down to sleep, Wilf went outside. Night had fallen – but not darkness. The housing estate was bathed in a lavender-coloured light, as if someone had left the television on all night in the sky. There was a damp chill and a faint lingering smell of burning plastic. He'd hate to live here – it was a horrible, boring place; there probably wasn't even a shop within walking distance. He wanted something to lift his spirits and bring him out of himself. He scrabbled around in the sand bucket by the front door until he found a cigarette butt that had barely been smoked. Taking a small folder of matches from his back pocket, he sat down on the front step, lit up and sucked hard.

The tip of his cigarette butt glowed. And some stars, low slung in the sky, glowed too. Were they really stars? Or real-*effect* stars? The night was so light. He looked around – all the other houses in the estate were empty, their windows dark. He squinted up again at those low stars. No, they were not stars. Aircraft lights or spotlights, more likely. The lights seemed to be moving slightly, wavering. Or maybe searching.

Wilf pressed his back against the door, took a long drag on the cigarette and peered into the distance. He told himself to stop imagining things. This was only a sort of night-time mirage. A trick of the light.

Or maybe a light that was not a light? Those men weren't just killers. They were smart, techie killers. Crog said that they had always had the best weapons. Why should it be any different today? Smart weapons meant radars, probes, satellites, heat-seeking, bowl-seeking electronic things in the sky.

Wilf swore under his breath. He stamped out his cigarette and darted inside.

Crog and Ishbel were asleep. Ishbel was on her side, her hair neatly fanned out around her as if she were floating in water; Crog lay with his mouth unattractively open.

Wilf leaned over, averting his eyes from that terrible wrung neck. Crog's body was curled up round his bowl. Only it wasn't *his* bowl, was it? *Wilf* had nicked it. And it was *Wilf* who'd been chased. *Wilf* whose home had been wrecked. By rights, it was *Wilf*'s bowl really. *He* should have it.

Wilf peeled back Crog's arm and gently prised the box out. Quietly, quietly, he opened the lid and, trying not to let the foil crinkle, removed the bowl. He cupped his hands underneath and held it, just as other hands in other ages had held it. The wood was dry and smooth as a snake.

There is a certain happiness that comes from getting what you want in life. And for just a moment, Wilf felt simple, pure contentment.

He looked down into the bowl, and he listened to the soundlessness of the night outside, and his life was complete. Yet . . . Yet there was also something on the very edge of his hearing, just the thread of a voice calling out. And the sound, he knew, came from *beyond* outside. It was full of yearning. Wilf felt tears well up in his eyes.

He stroked the sides of the bowl. His fingers came upon the small fissure in the wood.

He turned the bowl over. The crack ran down the side of the bowl, widening into a dark little delta at the base. A tiny, slender triangle of wood about half a centimetre wide was missing. He held the bowl up to his eyes. With only the light from the fire, it was hard to see if the crack was recent. But it didn't seem to be, and certainly the edge wasn't snagging. He could just fit the tip of his little finger into the crevice.

'Thief!' Crog was glaring at him.

'What's your problem? I just wanted to have a look,' said Wilf.

'Give it me back!' In the firelight Crog's irises were tawny, like a lion's.

'There's a chip . . . What happened?'

Crog didn't reply. He was crouching now, ready to jump on him.

'OK, OK,' said Wilf unsoothingly. 'Keep your hair on. I'm not going to steal it.'

'The bowl!' Crog's arms were outstretched. His eyes didn't leave Wilf's face. 'Give it me back!'

Wilf sighed. He held out the bowl and Crog took it. Slowly and carefully, as if cradling a baby, he put it back in the box, tucked it in with foil and clicked the lid shut.

'What happened to the bowl, then?' asked Wilf. 'How come it's cracked?'

'I failed afore. I cannot fail—'

'Oh, don't start that again. You're like a stuck disc.'

'A disc?'

'Never mind. Forget it,' said Wilf. 'But why won't you let me hold the bowl?'

'Holding is akin to having. Only the bearers hold, and that is a task – a sacred task that in my time fell upon me. I was the bearer. I would go out on the nights when the old moon lay abed. Then, when the time of the tides came, I would go down to the shore and pour our honey and mead into the bowl. Then I would walk out into the cold, black water carrying the bowl aloft. And the darkness covered me and the water pulled at my feet, and when the time was right and the sweet and the salt water turned, at that very time I would pour out the good things from the bowl. The night would be my witness and the stars in the sky would deepen and the west wind lift and the grey wolves on the mountain would howl.'

'Crikey,' murmured Wilf, his chest and arms all goose bumps now. Then he added, 'But no wolves now? Eh, Crog?'

'Different wolves. Their coats have changed,' he replied, looking sharply at Wilf.

Wilf grinned at Crog. Crog did not grin back. Instead he lay down on his side, facing away from Wilf, and pulled up his knees so that his body curved up round the box.

Eventually he said, 'The bowl . . . Never steal the bowl. Make a vow.'

Wilf did not reply.

'Make a vow,' repeated Crog.

'OK,' said Wilf tiredly. 'I promise. Whatever.'

CHAPTER 11

Wilf opened his eyes. It only took a moment for him to recall everything: Crog. The bowl. The journey. *Them*.

He staggered to his feet. Ishbel was still asleep by the fire. But there was no Crog. No box.

Wilf picked up the bedcovers by the fire. No Crog. He moved all the cushions as if he were looking for a mislaid mobile or a wallet, not a person. But there was still no Crog.

'Crog!' Wilf staggered over to the bathroom. It was empty.

He opened the front door. Outside there were only the empty houses, and the neat little squares of grass.

Where could he have gone?

Wilf swore vilely under his breath.

When he came back into the sitting room, Ishbel was sitting up.

'He hasn't gone, has he?' she asked.

'I've looked everywhere,' said Wilf.

Ishbel's face had a bare, scraped look. 'Maybe *they*

came for him in the night. But there's no sign of a break-in. And we'd know all about it, wouldn't we?'

'No we wouldn't,' said Wilf. 'We wouldn't know about anything. 'Cos we'd be *dead* – like Jenkins. And before we were dead we'd be—'

'OK, OK,' said Ishbel. 'But why? Why'd he run off like that?'

Wilf paused. Reluctantly he replied, 'We had this thing last night.'

'*Thing?*' Ishbel folded her arms.

'About the bowl. After you were asleep he sort of woke up. I wasn't meaning to take it off him. I only wanted to hold it.'

'You tried to take his bowl?'

'Why not? It's not his. It's *me* that got it,' replied Wilf.

'No wonder he's done a runner,' said Ishbel.

Wilf ignored her.

'How's he going to survive?' she continued. 'He won't last a minute out there. If we find him dead in a pool of blood, it'll be your fault.'

'He's dead already,' retorted Wilf. 'Nobody lives for three thousand years.'

'*Is* he dead?' said Ishbel tiredly. 'I don't understand what's going on. I don't know who he is. Or why we're here. How *can* he be dead anyway?'

'You saw that screen in the station. He wasn't there. He's here, but yet . . . I dunno.'

'Come on,' said Ishbel. 'We'd better go and look for him.'

It was early. They drove around the empty housing development – there was no one, not even a cat, in sight. Wilf turned into the street leading to the retail park. Here too things were pretty dead, with most of the metal shutters on the units still down.

Where could Crog go in a place like this?

They were driving slowly now, looking left and right, inspecting the front porches of small factories. Ishbel spotted a couple of workmen in hard hats coming out of a car park holding paper cups and Styrofoam takeaway boxes.

Wilf turned into the car park and drew up beside a long wooden shack with a cardboard sign above the door saying KOFFEE POT. The air smelled of frying bacon.

The café was warm and noisy, with a television on in one corner and several groups of workmen sitting down to enormous tea-fuelled breakfasts. Crog was at a table at the back. He had a large plate of chips in front of him, along with an unopened can of alcohol-free lager.

He glanced up when they came in, then took a chip

between forefinger and thumb, dipped it first in the ketchup, then in the brown sauce, then in his mouth.

'I told you to use a fork,' said Ishbel, standing over him.

Crog looked at her balefully and stuffed the rest of the chip into his mouth.

Wilf and Ishbel sat down. Crog pulled his plate nearer and tucked the lager into a side pocket of the photographer's waistcoat. The box was on the chair beside him.

'What did you do that for, Crog?' asked Ishbel. 'You can't just disappear like that.'

'Hungry,' replied Crog sulkily. He didn't look at Wilf.

'We didn't know where you were! And how did you know what to ask for? You didn't say *Big root fingers in fat*, did you?'

'I said *Chips*,' said Crog stiffly. 'And, *Please*.'

'And how were you going to pay, anyway?'

'Card.' Crog tapped the breast pocket of his waistcoat.

'Thanks,' said Ishbel coldly. She leaned over and took the card back.

'You were going to put a plate of chips on a *debit card*!' exclaimed Wilf. 'That's ridiculous!'

'No,' Crog corrected him. '*Three* plates.'

'Nice of you to think of us,' said Ishbel.

But Crog shook his head and pointed to two dirty

plates on the table. Both had little telltale pools of red and brown. 'I gave me three plates,' he said, stroking his belly.

'He's got a point,' said Wilf. 'We don't know when we'll eat next.'

The waitress came over to take their orders and caught sight of the box sitting on the chair. 'Hello! What's this we've got here?' she said in that voice women reserve for babies and puppies.

'CDs,' said Wilf quickly.

'Really? With breathing holes?'

'OK, it's a hamster. We didn't know if pets were allowed in here.'

'Awww,' said the waitress.

'Brindled back, white paws,' Wilf added quickly.

'Aww! Let's have a look.'

'Sorry,' said Ishbel. 'It's nocturnal.' She shut the menu firmly. 'We'll have two full breakfasts, but forget the fried bread.'

'Anything more for your little brother?' asked the waitress.

'No,' said Ishbel, looking sternly at Crog. 'He's had quite enough already.'

When the waitress had taken away Crog's dirty plates, Ishbel paid with her card and spread the road map out on the table.

'Where next?' she asked. 'Do we have a long way to go?'

Crog nodded.

'How far?'

'Three long summer days of walking,' replied Crog.

'Which way?'

Crog pointed to the front of the café.

'I'd say that's north,' said Wilf.

Ishbel pointed to a nodule of blue veins on the map. 'Look, Crog. This is where we are.'

But Crog turned his head away.

'Think of it this way, Crog,' said Wilf. 'You are looking on the land from above. Like a hawk flying overhead. This is what you see. Those lines are roads.'

Crog glanced scornfully at the map. 'Where are the trees and the stones? Hawks see mice. They see stoats and coneys.'

'Look!' said Ishbel, tracking the lines on the map with her forefinger. 'There only are two roads north from here, and only one of them leads northwest, which is where he wants to go.'

'We take the road of the hooded crow,' pronounced Crog.

'Roads nowadays don't have names. They have numbers. What's this crow road like?'

'Dark,' said Crog. 'Trees and black shadow overhead.

Mountains on the heart side. Water to your spear side.'

Ishbel looked at the map again. 'Yup, that's it!' she said triumphantly, jabbing at a red line. 'We'll take the A82. That goes up the west side of a loch. And there are hills on the other side.'

Two vast oval plates arrived piled high with fried food.

Crog shook his head in wonder. 'A whole egg of a hen for one man!'

'Yeah,' said Wilf, bursting the yolk with his fork.

'A whole egg of a hen for you *alone* to eat,' said Crog, his voice nearly a whisper now.

'Of course. Everyone eats *whole* eggs. What's the matter with you? What kind of hole did you come from!'

'Hole?' Crog looked offended. 'Not a hole. A hut.'

'Don't listen to him, Crog,' said Ishbel. 'And do stop staring. I can't eat with your eyes drilling into my plate. You can have my black pudding as long as you keep your mouth shut when you chew.'

Wilf was chasing a last button mushroom around his plate when Ishbel gave a little cry of shock.

He followed her gaze to the television and saw a view of Wilmot Towers, with ticker tape cordoning off the entrance and two policeman standing guard. The screen changed to a press conference. Their father, his eyes red and his face looking crumpled, was sitting behind a long desk with police officers on either side of him. One of the policemen was reading a statement – but over the noise in the café Wilf couldn't hear anything. Then their father spoke, his eyes beseeching the camera. Wilf strained his ears, but the waitress was shouting an order to the kitchen. One thing Wilf *did* know – his father wasn't just talking to a crowd; he was addressing *them*, here, in this very café. He had never seen his dad look so desperate before. *He thinks he's lost all his family now*, he thought. *And maybe he has*.

Wilf shook his head, partly to get a grip of himself and partly – though he knew this was idiotic – to try and shake out that last thought.

'Look what we've done to him,' said Ishbel in a low voice.

'We go now,' said Crog, thrusting a handful of sugar sachets into his waistcoat pocket.

Wilf ignored him. 'We'll have to call Dad and put his mind at rest.'

'We go now. *Please*,' insisted Crog.

Ishbel turned to Wilf. 'How can we call him? I know he looks terrible – like he does on Mum's anniversary. But what can we say? We can't reassure him. We're not safe ourselves.'

CHAPTER 12

They skirted round Glasgow and through the commuter villages lying in the shadow of the Campsie Fells. Wilf drove fast, crouched over the steering wheel, his eyes moving between the road and the rear-view mirror. But there was no silver Mercedes.

At the head of a loch they hit holiday land: campsites, marinas down by the shore, and little leisure boats bobbing in the water. They also came upon the spring bank holiday traffic.

The road followed the winding contours of the loch, and they were stuck behind a camper van. At every bend it almost came to a halt. Wilf drove close behind, flashing his headlights. The van didn't pull over.

They approached a campsite, Wilf praying that the van would turn off. That was his only hope – that and the remote possibility that the Mercedes was stuck behind a similar vehicle. But Badger probably had some little electronic gizmo that vaporized caravans.

The camper van didn't turn off – nor did it vaporize. Instead it just bumbled on.

Wilf tried again. He flashed his headlights and darted forward, pulling out to try and herd it off the road.

Crog, sitting in the back seat, pursed his lips and clutched the door handle.

Wilf ground back into first gear for yet another bend. 'Better in your day, eh?' he said. 'Must have been quicker when you could gallop down here on your white stallions . . .'

'We walked,' replied Crog shortly.

The fuel warning light flashed. Wilf sighed. How could the petrol run out so fast? That's what came of choosing an interesting old car and driving it hell for leather over bad roads. He hoped Ishbel wouldn't notice the light – she'd be sure to say he had only himself to blame.

'Is that the fuel light?' asked Ishbel.

'Yup.'

'But we've only just filled up. Must be something wrong. A leak in the fuel tank. You should have gone for something more ordinary.'

'Mm,' said Wilf.

'You've only got yourself to blame,' said Ishbel.

They came to a stretch of straight road lined with beech trees, and here at last Wilf swerved round the camper van and spurted forward into a tunnel of green light. There was nothing in his way now – and he had nothing to lose. He revved the engine and felt giddy and giggly with the speed.

'If we'd only had time,' said Ishbel, turning in her seat to look quizzically at Crog, 'I could have had a go at your hair. It's a bit dull and lifeless. Needs some product – a bit of serum for starters.'

Wilf snorted. Crog said nothing, but loudly.

'Thanks for the ringing endorsement, guys!' said Ishbel.

'You just come up with this stuff from nowhere, don't you? It's hardly the time!' said Wilf.

'It is *so* the time. When you crash the car – which is a dead cert, the way you're driving – it would be nice to be presentable corpses, don't you think? If we can't stretch to clean knickers, we should at least have shiny hair.'

'Speak for yourself,' said Wilf primly.

They continued along the loch, passing the turnoff to Kintyre and then a huge turreted hotel. Soon they'd left it behind, and found themselves in a long rising valley covered in pale grass.

Wilf looked in the rear-view mirror. Still no Mercedes.

But Crog's eyes were flickering uneasily.

'What's up, Crog?' he asked.

'I know this land,' said Crog. 'There is a river here with falling water. But where are the woods?'

'They're up there.' Ishbel pointed up the hillside towards a large rectangular plantation of pine and spruce, crisscrossed with fire paths.

Crog looked at the slab of dark green and shook his head. 'No.' He winced. 'No. *True* woods.'

Wilf pulled into a petrol station. While Ishbel and Crog went off to find a toilet, he put twenty pounds worth of fuel in the tank, went into the shop and queued up at the counter to pay. He kept his head down – he could see the security camera above the till.

In Ishbel's purse there were two £20 notes, a £10 note and £4.29 in small change. His hand was just reaching out for some bars of fudge when he caught sight of the pile of newspapers on the counter.

His heartbeat snagged. The headline at the foot of the page said, MURDER IN WAPPING PENTHOUSE! BANKER'S CHILDREN MISSING. Underneath was a hazy passport photograph of Jenkins, and a bigger, formal family portrait of Ishbel and Wilf with their father. The photograph had been taken a few years ago: Ishbel had plaits and Wilf looked goofy, with his new front teeth still too big for his face. That was the last photograph of the three of them together. Almost the last time, Wilf thought bitterly, that the three of them *had* been together.

He scanned the rest of the newsstand. The story was everywhere; the tabloids had even got hold of his police mug shots.

He handed the money to the cashier. She looked at him and said slowly, 'Could you wait a minute? I've just got to replace the till roll.' Then she turned and headed through the door to the back of the shop.

Wilf pocketed the bars of fudge and hurried out.

Ishbel was waiting by the car with Crog.

'Get in. Quick! They're on to us,' said Wilf.

They screeched out of the petrol station onto the road north. The land ahead was bare, with just a few gorse bushes in bloom. So no cover here.

'*Who* is on to us?' asked Ishbel.

'Police,' said Wilf.

'How d'you know? I didn't see any around.'

'The cashier – she recognized me. She went out the back to call them. We're all over the newspapers.'

'I'll never get into medical school now,' said Ishbel. There was a pause, then she added, 'What was I wearing in the photos?'

'Nothing. You had nothing on,' said Wilf solemnly.

'Except for a pink hair band. You'll never, *ever* get into medical school now.'

'Stop it!' Ishbel's eyes were welling. '*I* didn't get us into all this.'

'Nor did I,' retorted Wilf.

'Yes you did!'

'Only in part. It's mostly thanks to our little amigo in the back.'

Wilf glanced over his shoulder. Crog was sitting quietly, his eyes fixed on the window.

The road was getting busier. Wilf overtook a stream of cars and swerved back to his own side just before a bend. The engine juddered at such high speed. Maybe if he slowed down a little, that twenty pounds of fuel might get them further. *How far now?* he wondered.

'Two long days walking on the low lands,' said Crog.

'Sorry?' said Wilf with a start. 'Don't creep me out! I wasn't talking to you.'

Crog shrugged and sucked at his teeth. 'But only a night and a day over the high passes.' He paused. 'Yet the west wind cold as death.'

'Then shouldn't we take the low lands?' said Wilf. Though he didn't much like the look of the valley. This wasn't his kind of place. They were on a lonely road – scrubby brown moorland and heather and black tarns as far as the eye could see. And boulders. Huge granite boulders scattered everywhere, as if a giant had dropped a bag of grey peas from a great height.

'This road,' said Ishbel, 'somehow seems awfully familiar.'

Wilf floored the accelerator, but the car would go no faster.

A few miles further on, the road curved to the west. Ahead of them was a long valley scooped out between two mountain ridges. It was very bare – just a thin vein of road along the bottom, with a skyline of jagged black rocks; there were traces of snow still lying in the crevices.

Ishbel had the map on her knees. 'There's ten miles of this valley. No roads off. Nothing. Once we're in, there's no way out.'

'Where's the nearest town?' asked Wilf.

'Fort William. Five miles beyond the end of the valley.'

'They'll send police down and set up a checkpoint and catch us all like rats in a barrel.'

'Then take the turning coming up on the left,' said Ishbel. 'That's our only chance.'

'No!' hissed Crog. '*They* know this land. They will be lying in wait.'

'But we have to, matey,' said Wilf. 'If we stay in this valley, we'll be heading straight for the police roadblock.'

He looked left, and saw that the turning Ishbel meant was merely a farm track. 'Look – they won't want to risk their precious Mercedes on that. It would wreck the suspension.'

He turned off, and the car bumped along the narrow dirt road, heading southwest, away from the valley. A spidery little hand clutched at his shoulder.

'No! No! No!' said Crog. His huge eyes were swimming in the rear-view mirror.

'Get off! I'm driving.' Wilf shrugged the hand off his shoulder and, in his distraction, took the next rise too fast; the metal undercarriage screeched as it scraped the ground.

He leaned forward over the steering wheel and fixed his eyes on the mountain ahead. Crog was whimpering in the back, but as they approached the next bend, this became a high-pitched keening sound.

'Hey!' cried Ishbel. 'He's been right before! Let's go back!'

Wilf stopped the car. He couldn't summon the energy to deal with Crog *and* Ishbel. Instead he wound down the window. A damp breeze breathed against his cheek. He shut his eyes and inhaled deeply. That's what he needed. Time out. Fresh air. Yet there was a catch in his throat. The air was not as fresh as he'd expected. Cigar smoke . . . He sniffed again. *That* cigar smoke.

Ishbel grabbed his arm. *They* were here already – waiting somewhere nearby. Maybe just over the brow of the hill.

Wilf reversed back down the slope. At the first passing place, he turned the car round and accelerated back down the track, bumping and scraping and shuddering along.

'Are they behind us?' He couldn't bear to look in the mirror.

'Nobody there,' said Ishbel. 'I never thought you had such a good nose, Wilf.'

'Not as good as Crog's,' he replied.

Crog rubbed his eyes and smiled wanly. 'Thank you.' There was a slight pause, then he added experimentally, '*Matey.*'

Wilf turned back onto the main road along the valley. It followed the course of a small river. Two ragged ridges of rock hung high above them.

They passed two car parks where tour buses were spilling out tourists with hats and binoculars. Ishbel grimaced. 'Who'd want to come here by choice?'

'Something comes,' said Crog.

Wilf strained his ears – and heard a very faint drone. Then a louder sound. Engines. The drone was getting louder and more insistent, reverberating along the floor of the valley. Whatever it was was coming up behind them very fast.

A biker on a huge Harley Davidson roared past the car. Then came a second bike, and a third. A fourth. A fifth. Then more and more. A score of bikers driving past, fast as machine-gun fire.

Ishbel gave a little laugh of relief.

Wilf drove on. A white van coming towards them flashed its lights in warning. Then another car flashed them. There had to be something up ahead: most likely a police checkpoint hidden round one of the bends.

Wilf had never – consciously – driven into the arms of the law before, and he wasn't going to make an exception now. At the next car park he pulled in. Another coach was disgorging elderly tourists, and a piper in full Highland regalia was tuning his drones nearby. Tourists were bunched around him.

'We have to think of *something* . . .' Wilf said.

He noticed a four-wheel-drive parked nearby. Maybe they could cling to the undercarriage? No, Ishbel would never agree to that.

He looked doubtfully at the coach. Could they hide away in the toilets?

Ishbel followed his gaze. 'But how would we get past

the driver? He'll be sitting in there with his newspaper. He's not going to move.'

There must be *something*.

Then Ishbel said tiredly, 'Go on, Crog. Save our lives again.'

And Crog replied, 'I know the ways.'

CHAPTER 13

Crog was out of the car in a trice. With the box under his arm, he quickly skirted the crowd of tourists and the piper, and took off down a sheep track that led across the bottom of the valley. He didn't look back.

Wilf and Ishbel dashed after him and found him sitting on a boulder in a clump of alders. He had replaced the box in the rucksack and was now hauling the straps over his shoulders. He sprang to his feet. 'Fast, fast.'

'Where're we going?' asked Wilf.

Crog pointed south down the valley to a small wooded track that ran up the hill beside a river. And before Wilf had time to catch his breath, Crog took off again, following the path over a little footbridge and up into a narrow gully.

The ascent was steep and strewn with boulders. Crog, fast and sure-footed, hurried upwards, never stopping. Wilf came behind, his eyes on Crog's skinny white legs – so puny but so much more effective than his own.

Soon the car park was far behind them. Wilf continued

up, with the sound of the river at his side. Yet there was another, fainter sound too: of light footsteps.

He glanced round. Ishbel, red-faced and panting, was some twenty metres behind him, but this sound was nearer. Was it the patter of raindrops? But there was no rain. The rustle of leaves in the wind? No. It couldn't be.

The sky was grey now, as if the light had been sucked out of it. But there was no sign of anyone following them up the gully. Wilf sniffed. No tobacco smoke. The air was pure and cool.

Pitter-patter. Pitter-patter.

It was feet.

Wilf closed his eyes . . . Definitely feet.

Trick of the wind?

But the sound was very close. Too close. Almost as if it were *inside* his mind.

He started humming to block out the sound. Whenever he stopped, the footsteps returned.

Then the rain *did* start – just as a smattering of drops at first; but suddenly the sky seemed to heave, and sheets of water poured down, beating the grass flat.

Wilf followed the path upwards, rain dripping off his nose.

Pitter-patter. Pitter-patter.

Some way further on, the gully became shallower and the river, strewn with rocks, slowed and widened. Crog crossed over, jumping from rock to rock. He made it look easy.

But of course it wasn't. Wilf stopped on each rock, his feet slipping as he tried to regain his balance. By the time he reached the far side, Crog was out of sight again.

The path, now slimy with rain, wove on upwards. At last Wilf clambered up over a lip of rock and came out at the top of the gully. He bent over to catch his breath. He was now looking down – not on the far side of the mountain, but on a small, shallow valley some seven metres below. Nothing much grew here; there was just grey scree and boulders and a couple of wizened trees.

And, hunched over in the lee of one of the boulders, was Crog.

Wilf joined him. There wasn't much space, but at least they were out of the rain.

'The rain is good. We leave no scent,' said Crog. 'The valley is hidden – you see nothing from below. Here we stay a time. After the rain, we go west, towards the resting sun.'

'I thought we were being followed when we came up,' said Wilf; the smell of wet Crog filled his nostrils. 'I heard footsteps – I didn't know what it was. Did you hear anything?'

'The rain,' said Crog, his eyes narrowing. 'I heard rain.'

'No. This wasn't rain. This was something else. People running . . . many people.'

At last Crog spoke. 'Last night you were holding the bowl. You trespassed on the dead. Be thankful it was only footsteps you heard. Not voices.'

'What! So they're ghosts, then? Or semi-ghosts – like you . . .' Wilf felt fearful, but intrigued as well. 'And what's so wrong with that? Why can't we hear what they say? I'm curious. Wouldn't it be interesting?'

Crog just shook his head and gave a little shudder.

Soon afterwards Ishbel arrived and squeezed in beside them, her hair dripping. She took off her ankle boots and started rubbing her toes.

Wilf felt in his pocket and brought out one of the bars of fudge. He broke off two squares for each of them. Crog sniffed his fudge and put it in his mouth. A second later he gave a gasp of pain and clutched his jaw.

'That'll be the sweetness biting into his cavities,' said Ishbel. 'Wilf, let that be a lesson to you in oral hygiene.'

Wilf looked at the pointy ends on Ishbel's boots. 'You can't talk, with those stupid boots. Where are your toes supposed to go?'

'Blisters,' she said, 'are the price of fashion.'

Wilf watched her wiggle her painfully pink toes. 'At least we're safe here,' he said consolingly. 'It's a hidden valley.'

'We're not safe at all,' she said miserably. 'When the car park empties tonight, the police will spot the car and put two and two together. They'll follow us. They could bring dogs. Or helicopters.'

'They won't,' said Wilf. 'Not tonight. They won't start till nine o'clock tomorrow morning – even though we're minors. If they begin any earlier, they'll be paying overtime and they never like doing that.'

'That's just the kind of detail you *would* know, isn't it?' said Ishbel. 'But there's still those men.'

Wilf put his arm round her. They sat in silence for a while, and he listened again. No footsteps now – just the drumming of the rain.

Crog's eyes followed the flight of a bird of prey back and forth across the sky. Eventually he announced, 'We go now.'

'It's still raining,' said Wilf. 'Why don't we wait a bit?'

'Storms will be upon us . . .' Crog looked up at the clouds over the far ridge.

'How do you know?' asked Ishbel. 'The sky always looks grey in Scotland.'

'Crog can probably just feel it in his bones,' said Wilf. 'Can't you, Crog?'

'Storms come,' said Crog. 'The peregrine tells me.'

'Now, isn't that poetic!' said Ishbel.

Crog blinked at her. 'The peregrine is hunting under rain. No bird likes to hunt on wet wings. And yet she hunts. She stores up against bad weather riding in on the north wind. We go *now*.'

'Well, don't just run off this time,' said Ishbel. 'Where are we going?'

Crog pointed to the western side of the valley: the lower part was a steep slope of scree; above stood a sheer black rock face.

'That's a cliff! I can't do that!' Ishbel's voice wobbled.

Crog ran at the scree, scrambled up and hoisted himself onto a small ledge that marked the foot of the cliff. Then he started the climb, clutching at tiny crevices in the rock.

Ishbel approached the scree gingerly. Halfway up, her feet began to slide back, sending loose stones raining down behind her. She let out a little wail and slid downwards, landing at the bottom with her front covered in black dust.

'Run at it – you need some momentum,' urged Wilf.

Ishbel sniffed and wiped her face. She stepped back

and ran at the scree. This time she just made the ledge and scrambled up.

Wilf followed, noting as he did so that there was no sound of footsteps now, just a faint drumroll of wind. He pulled himself up onto the ledge, where Ishbel was crouching with her head in her knees.

'I'm filthy now,' she said.

Wilf looked at the black rock above them. Crog was some way up, the bottom of his kaftan flapping in the wind. He was moving fast. A four-legged spider.

'Come on, Ishie,' said Wilf. 'You can't give up now! Not before you've fallen and broken your neck.'

Ishbel still didn't open her eyes. 'You're not even funny. And don't tell me not to look down.'

Wilf gave her arm a squeeze. 'You're taller than Crog. If he can reach the handholds, you can too. Come on, Ishie. Get up.'

He held her arm and she got uncertainly to her feet, then leaned back against the rock face, her eyes tight shut.

'Ishie, you can do it,' he told her. 'You *know* you can – even in those boots. This rock won't come away in your hand. I've climbed drainpipes that are worse.'

'I bet you have,' she replied.

She shuffled round to face the cliff and, agonizingly

slowly, set off. Sometimes her legs shook, and sometimes she froze, but gradually she edged her way up the cliff. Wilf followed. He climbed steadily, and when at last he pulled himself over the last ledge, Ishbel grasped him by the arm and helped him.

They were on the summit now, standing in a scouring wind with the valleys cast before them. Far away to the south, beyond the shoulder of the mountain, lay a long tongue of still blue water. To the north was the car park where they had left the Saab. Wilf could see other tiny cars moving like little beads along a winding string of road.

He ducked his head, but Ishbel laughed. 'We're pinpricks to them,' she said.

They crouched down out of the wind. The ridge was directly ahead of them. In places the way was marked by a narrow line of rocks and boulders running along the very top of the mountain. On either side the ground fell away sharply.

'You call *that* a path?' said Wilf.

Crog made a fist, held it out to him and ran a finger along his grubby knuckles. Then he nodded to the ridge. 'Crog,' he said.

'What do you mean? Talk English,' said Ishbel.

'We call this road the Crog. The way of the clenched hand. It is a hard walk.'

'But *you* are Crog, aren't you . . .' Wilf was puzzled.

'Crog means *hand*,' said Crog. 'Not just *hand*, *clawed hand. Grasping hand. Claw. Paw. Fist.*'

'Fist – that's a good name!'

'Yeah, but *grasping hand* isn't quite so good,' observed Ishbel.

Crog pointed to the knuckle of his forefinger. 'We are here and' – he indicated the knuckle of his little finger – '*here* we find shelter. We go now, before the storm is upon us.'

They set off along the ridge in single file: Crog at the front, quick-footed and deft; then Ishbel; Wilf bringing up the rear. The way was very narrow and Wilf knew he shouldn't look down – yet the path wound to and fro so he had to watch where he put his feet. If he tripped, he'd fall a very long way and be smashed on the rocks below.

How was Ishbel doing? He didn't know. He could hear her breathing hard and letting out an occasional sob. But she kept going.

They scrambled down into the first dip and then up onto the second knuckle of the ridge. The sky was slowly turning leaden and the wind was quickening. Wilf's ears burned with cold, and his fingers were numb.

Later, they stopped in a small hollow where a huge lichen-covered rock sheltered them from the wind. Ishbel crumpled to the ground and took off her boots. The skin on her toes and the backs of her heels was raw and bleeding. She rocked back and forth, lips pursed, tears coursing down her cheeks.

Crog tore a strip of material off the hem of his kaftan. Then he disappeared behind one of the rocks. A minute later he returned and crouched down in front of Ishbel. In his hand was a folded piece of the material, now very damp. Very gently he dabbed at her raw toes.

Ishbel winced.

He smiled up at her with his terrible teeth and said in a reassuring voice, 'Soon we are finding some moss.'

She leaned over, sniffed suspiciously and then jerked her head back. 'That's *pee*! Crog! You peed on that bit of stuff, and now you're *touching* me with it!'

Crog smiled. He was pressing the material against the tender sides of her little toes. 'The pain goes? No?'

'*No!*' said Ishbel, pushing him away. 'It's *gross*! You've just pissed on my feet!'

Wilf laughed. 'Wee is meant to be acidic. He's just cleaning your wounds. It's Stone Age medicine for you. Don't look so cross. You'll hurt his feelings.'

'What about *my* feelings? And *my* feet!' she cried.

'Come on! You've got to laugh. Look on the bright side . . .' said Wilf.

'What *bright side*? We're stuck up a freezing mountain, the police are looking for us, and we are being hunted by murderers. I'm starving. My feet are torn to shreds and, oh yeah, some savage has just pissed on me! So where precisely is this *bright side*?'

'Well,' said Wilf, 'you could be dead already, couldn't you?'

Ishbel narrowed her eyes at him.

'Better here,' murmured Crog. 'Better here than . . .'

'Better here than where, Crog?' she asked.

He paused for a moment, then got to his feet and said firmly, 'Beyond. Better here than beyond.'

'What's beyond like? Why's it worse?' asked Wilf.

But Crog had already set off again and he didn't turn back.

They plodded on, the wind blowing so hard that Ishbel's hair flared above her head and Wilf couldn't look up without shielding his eyes. Eventually they made their way down into the final dip, and up onto the last and steepest of the 'knuckles'. The light was going – leaching the last of the colour from the bracken on the hillsides and turning all the land an eerie monochrome.

They stopped to rest on the last peak. The mountains seemed to bulk up in the dusk, and to the west they could see the coast, where the sun dipped down into a black sea.

In the valley below, the cars had their headlights on. Wilf peered down at the car park at the far end of the valley. Here there were more lights – some of them blue and flashing. The flying squad would be scouring the land.

Crog nudged Wilf and pointed to his ears. But Wilf could hear nothing over the howl of the wind. He counted the blue lights down in the valley: one, two, three, four, *five* cars. They were taking this seriously. Very seriously. He shouted to Ishbel, 'They'll have helicopters out in the morning.'

'No, they won't,' she shouted back.

'Why not?' he asked.

Ishbel pointed north into the darkening sky.

CHAPTER 14

I shbel was right: two helicopters were out already. They rose up over the far side of the valley in a flurry of lights. One veered east, sweeping down towards the car park; the other hovered above the mountainside. Wilf could see the police markings, painted in a toxic shade of yellow on the cabin roofs.

He crouched down behind the rock, but Crog pulled at his jacket. Wilf tried to shake him off. 'We can't go now!' he hissed. 'There's no cover! They'll see us.'

'We are close!' said Crog. And he set off downhill, dodging between the rocks.

Ishbel said, 'It's nearly dark. They won't see us. We'll freeze if we stay here.' And she followed Crog.

Wilf thought, *They will see us for sure. And if they can't, they'll have thermal imaging anyway*. But he hurried after her.

Then the rain took hold in earnest – cold shafts of water coming down at a slant, drenching every part of Wilf. He followed Ishbel down a slope of black scree, leaning back on his heels and letting the stones take him. But the scree skidded faster and faster, and he went with it. In the end he could only stop by running straight into the trunk of a pine tree. The spiky branches tore at his face.

Wilf looked around. There was just a smattering of trees; it was mainly gorse and rocks. Ishbel was getting to her feet nearby.

'Where's Crog?' he asked.

She pointed. 'He went that way, but I can't see him now.'

They ran on. Wilf stumbled, and suddenly saw that Ishbel had left the path and swerved round some rocks. Was she shouting? He could hear nothing above the wind and the rain.

The helicopter over the ridge was peeling away from the mountainside. It was coming their way now.

Wilf made for the rocks and found Ishbel bending down over a hole in the ground. It wasn't an animal lair – just a round hole between two boulders. It seemed to be a straight drop, like a mineshaft.

'He's down there,' she said. 'I heard him whistle . . . Crog? Are you there?'

'I am,' called a tiny echoey voice. 'Come, come!'

'How? I can't see where I'm going.'

'Just get in!' said Wilf. The helicopter was moving faster. Soon it would be overhead.

Ishbel faltered.

'Hurry!'

Finally she lowered her legs into the hole. Now only her head and shoulders were above ground. 'My feet aren't touching anything!' she said.

'Just let go!'

'But how far is it? It could be miles!'

'*Let go!*' shouted Wilf.

She wouldn't.

There was nothing for it. He stood over her and pushed her drenched shoulders down hard. Her arms flailed, and then, in a flash, she was gone.

Wilf didn't wait. He clambered into the hole after her, shut his eyes and didn't give himself time to think. He just let go.

The hole spat him through darkness. He didn't have time to worry before hitting the bottom; the shock ran up his body like a flame and he crumpled onto his side.

'Broken anything?' asked Ishbel, almost hopefully.

Wilf opened his eyes into darkness. Not complete darkness: far above him, the hole let in one faint bore of light. The walls of the cave folded away into shadow. There was no wind, and no sound of the rain, just gentle dripping noises and, somewhere nearby, a faint scrabbling.

He closed his eyes again, hoping for sleep. His feet and shins felt pulpy.

Ishbel shook him. 'Sit up. You're not road kill!'

'Bad landing,' he muttered.

'At least you had warning!' said Ishbel. 'I think I've broken a rib. Thanks for that! Remind me to push you down the next cliff we meet. Lucky I rolled out of the way, wasn't it? A second later and you'd have squashed me flat.'

'My pleasure,' said Wilf. 'But where are we? It smells like a church in here.'

Ishbel sniffed. 'Hmm, it's that kind of air, isn't it? Blimey, it's cold!'

'And where's Crog?'

'You can hear him – he's rootling around somewhere nearby.'

Wilf took a small, damp book of matches out of his pocket. Again and again he struck the damp, bendy matches. Finally he got a flame and held the match till it burned his fingers. Now he could see that the cave walls were marbled with swirls of brown and cream rock. By the far wall was a small pool of black water. Everything – the walls, the rocks, the little piles of animal bones on the ground – shone with moisture, like a cold steam room.

Wilf looked up at the hole they'd fallen through. Was it five metres away? Eight? They were safe from the helicopters – no police-issue thermal imager would pick them up here.

'It's like one of those bottle-shaped dungeons they used to throw prisoners in and leave them to starve,' said Ishbel. Something about the cave was making her speak in a hushed voice.

Wilf looked around but could see no openings. He struck another match. Still no passageway. Nothing.

'Crog, how do we get out?'

Crog was over by the pool, scratching at the ground with a stone. He made a crowing noise at the back of his throat.

'Crog! *How do we get out?*' Wilf's voice boomed back across the wet walls.

But Crog just beamed at him and held up something that looked like a pointed tusk, curved like a scythe.

'Never mind that now, Crog. How are we going to get out?' Wilf repeated.

Crog pointed to the black pool and smiled again. 'Big breath!'

'I don't get it . . .'

'He wants us to dive. It'll be like the U-bend in a toilet,' said Ishbel tonelessly. 'You dive down and into a hole and hope you make it out the other end.'

'I still don't understand . . .'

Of course he understood. He thought there was nothing worse in life than creeping through holes. Well, there *was* something worse: creeping through *underwater* holes. He'd rather just die here in the cave. If they could only find a way to make a fire and warm up. Maybe some delicious animal would drop down through the hole and they could have a roast.

'What's not to understand?' said Ishbel. 'The way out is a tunnel somewhere in the pool. Crog's clearly done it before. And he hasn't got gills – or at least, I don't think he has.'

Wilf shut his eyes. This would be so much worse than the laundry shaft.

'There again,' Ishbel went on, 'that might be what he's hiding behind his rope.'

Wilf tried to rein in his panic and approach the matter slowly and calmly. He thought of Crog: Crog had narrow shoulders and a small head. He'd squeeze through any-thing. But what if the space was too small for proper-sized people?

'We'll die of hypothermia,' he concluded.

'No,' said Ishbel. 'We'll die of hypothermia if we stay here.'

Crog went first. Standing in the freezing pool by the cave wall, Ishbel and Wilf helped him thread his arms the wrong way through the rucksack straps so that the bag lay against his chest like a baby in a pouch. Then he bobbed down under the water and disappeared.

'It'll be pitch dark down there. We'll just have to follow where Crogsie went and then feel our way,' said Ishbel.

'You go first,' insisted Wilf.

'No,' she said, '*you* go.'

'Why me?'

''Cos otherwise you'll never do it.'

Wilf nodded. Of course she was right. He would never do it. Not an underwater tunnel. 'I wish he'd said how long the tunnel was.'

'Too late now. Just *go*!' said Ishbel.

And Wilf went. He dived down into the freezing water, and in a second he was through the gap in the cave wall and into an underground cavern; it was just wide enough for him to feel the sides if he stretched out his arms. Wilf swam through the darkness, his right hand out in front to feel his way along, his legs kicking frantically. The tunnel soon narrowed into a series of zigzags, the sides as rough as sandpaper. He swam on, feeling his way round the turns in the tunnel, his lungs expanding painfully to keep the air in. He came to a dead end and groped along the wall, skinning his palms in the process.

Ah! Not quite a dead end! There was an opening to the left, but it was tight. He wiggled one shoulder through and then the other. Suddenly his hand was touching something that was not rock. Something living! It shot away. Wilf gave a start and took in water. He choked and spluttered for a second.

What was it? One of those eyeless eel things that grab your arm and will never let go?

Don't think! *Move!*

He couldn't hold on any more. He kicked harder. When would this end? He felt above his head, vainly hoping that he might be through the tunnel. But the roof bearing down on him was still very much there. What would happen if he died? Would his skeleton just stay here or be washed away? No. There'd be no skeleton – it was so cold he probably wouldn't decompose.

He squirmed round yet another corner. The water was getting lighter now; he could make out shapes. The tunnel was widening.

He swam faster now that he didn't have to feel his way forward. He was light-headed, running on empty. Above him the roof of the tunnel rose and then vanished. Wilf rose too, his lungs burning.

A strong hand grasped his arm and pulled him upwards till his head broke through the surface. Spluttering horribly, he was dragged up onto a rocky ledge, where something hit him repeatedly in the small of the back. His head jerked pathetically as water and snot and bile spurted out. Then he sank into a puddle of his own making and, before darkness completely engulfed him, he noticed that his vomit was agreeably warm.

Chapter 15

Wilf opened his eyes. He was lying in a high-roofed cave, facing a huge crackling fire of heather and branches. His face was burning hot, and at the front, his clothes were crisp and dry, while his back still felt damp. On a nearby stone, Crog's photographer's waistcoat and Ishbel's boots and the contents of her little handbag lay steaming in the heat. Someone had taken off Wilf's trainers, and they too nestled close to the fire.

Crog was busy plaiting some pink fibres. Between his teeth he held the curved tusk he'd dug up earlier.

'Wilf!' said Ishbel, appearing through a narrow passageway carrying a huge bundle of brushwood. 'Well done! You've woken up now the work's finished. Crogsie and I have been hard at it since dawn!'

Her voice was unbearably cheerful. She always had been an early bird.

'Get up a minute,' she said.

Groggily Wilf stood up and she laid the brushwood on the stone where he'd been lying.

'What's that for?' he asked. 'Are you going to burn me too?'

'It's a mattress. A bog-myrtle mattress,' she said briskly. 'Crog's idea – keeps you warm at night, apparently. Smells nice, doesn't it? It's the only thing that does round here. You don't, that's for sure.' She nodded towards Crog. 'And nor does he.'

Wilf lay back down on the brushwood. It felt scratchy, but Ishbel was right – the smell was nice and herby.

She surveyed his bed with some satisfaction. 'It's quite fun, isn't it? The work keeps you warm. We're really playing house. Playing *cave*, I suppose.'

'What about the police?' asked Wilf.

'There's no sign of the helicopters yet, but it's early.'

'And what about *them*? Those blokes . . . Crog, if you know of this place, won't *they* know it too?'

'The valley people know black turf and marsh gas,' replied Crog. 'They know not the ways of the high hills.'

'But they're clever, aren't they?' said Ishbel. 'They've got those tracking gizmos. And that tool that just slices through metal fencing.'

Crog didn't look up. 'They're clever.' He shrugged. 'They have riches, but they know nothing.'

'And what are you doing?' asked Wilf. 'Isn't that Ishbel's belt you've got there?'

'It is.' Crog had taken the tusk out of his mouth and was slicing through the pink fibres.

'And . . .?'

'The girdle is strong and the twine will make a fine deer noose.'

'So, Ishie, you let him have it?' said Wilf. 'You've never let me borrow even a T-shirt!'

'Needs must,' she replied. 'Makes you want to weep, though, doesn't it? He can't know what he's wrecking. Gucci means nothing to him.'

Wilf could smell something savoury. He spotted a swollen brown lump of pastry lying on a stone by the fire. 'And what's that?' he asked.

'A chicken and mushroom pie,' said Ishbel. 'It's taking an age to dry out. Crog nicked it from the petrol station. That jacket of his has deep pockets.'

Ishbel prodded the waterlogged pastry. It leaked a cloudy fluid.

'So I'm not the only thief, eh?' Wilf grinned at Crog.

They ate messily, using their fingers to wipe up the gunge left on the stone. Afterwards Wilf felt he could have eaten another ten or twelve chicken and mushroom pies. If Ishbel hadn't been there, he'd have licked that stone.

Crog seemed revived by the tiny morsel of food. He

took off his scarf, scratched at the skin under the rope, then wound the scarf back round again.

Ishbel watched him with interest. She said, 'We can't have secrets now – not after all we've been through together. So why don't you tell us . . . What's that rope around your neck for? And why don't you take it off?'

Crog quickly looked down and picked up his work again.

'Cat got your tongue? Don't you think we deserve some sort of explanation?' said Ishbel.

He gave her an icy stare. Still he said nothing.

They sat in silence for a while. Crog was tying some small pieces of wood into his trap. His black, mangled little fingers were very deft.

Hearing faint scufflings coming from the dark corners of the cave, Wilf moved closer to the fire. What was it? Another sound in his mind? Or just mice? He peered into the gloom, but could see only darkness. He turned back to the fire and tried to think of other things. But someone, or something, breathed near his ear. He turned again. Nothing. Maybe it was just a draught.

'What's got into you?' asked Ishbel.

'Thought I heard something. Felt a chill . . .' Wilf rubbed the back of his neck.

'He *did* hear something,' said Crog, throwing a pile

of wood shavings onto the fire. The flames crackled.

Ishbel turned to Wilf. 'What did you hear?'

'A stoat,' he replied. 'I heard a stoat.'

Crog looked at him reproachfully. 'No stoat,' he said. 'The night before our last night, he took the bowl and he held it to his breast. Now he has ears to hear.'

'Of course I can *hear*! I've always been able to hear,' retorted Wilf.

Crog ignored him. 'The bowl has *power*. It gives us back the sounds we heard long ago: the creep of roots through the earth, the heartbeat of the linnet. The sounds of life and of death and of—' Suddenly he stopped.

'And of *what*?' asked Ishbel.

'Of beyond. The world of spirits. Not all shadows are silent.'

'Crog,' said Ishbel, almost in a whisper, 'do you mean *the dead*?'

'Aye,' said Crog, and returned to his plaiting.

Wilf shut his eyes, and the people he had known who had died drifted one by one into his mind. Jenkins – poor Jenkins. Mrs MacCullough, Dad's old housekeeper who'd had cancer. His old friend Stan, who'd played chicken on the railway line one time too many. Denzil, poor pathetic Denzil, who'd sniff or smoke or drink anything for kicks. And, of course, Mum. He thought of the yellow dress. He couldn't remember her face, but hadn't he once – he wished it was clearer – sat on her lap? And she'd had a big book all about a rabbit who wore trousers. And he had been so happy looking at the rabbit pictures. Hadn't his mother had tiny freckles on her forearms? He had found them so interesting. And she had turned the pages and been so very gentle. If she could only hold and love him now.

Wilf let out a long painful breath, almost a sob. He clenched his fists, pressing his nails into his palms. He *had* to get control. He was just tired from that swim through the tunnel. That was all.

He opened his eyes and saw that Crog was looking at him.

'Time will teach you,' Crog told him. 'The dead are always with us.'

When Crog had finished making the trap, they went along the passage and emerged high up on the mountain-side. With their backs pressed against the rocks, they scanned the morning sky and the grey-green arc of spruce and pine below.

There was nothing moving – no helicopters – and no sign of last night's storm. Just the far-off pale line of the shore and the blue sea beyond.

Crog pointed south to a narrow inlet where the loch they had seen earlier joined the sea. At the head of the loch stood a metal cantilevered bridge and a scattering of houses.

Suddenly Crog's outstretched arm dropped away. He seemed to slump. Staring down at the inlet, he said, 'A crabwalk!'

'What's up?' Wilf hadn't seen Crog upset before.

Crog looked at him furiously and hissed, 'You defile the falls!'

'What? The bridge?' said Wilf stupidly.

'Aye, that *crabwalk*!' spat Crog.

'We didn't do it personally,' said Ishbel.

Crog said nothing for a moment. Then, very quietly, he said, 'That's where we go, where the bowl must go. Into the falls, betwixt salt and sweet. When the tide turns.'

'We could get there today, if we stepped on it,' said Wilf.

'Wilf. It's *much* too far!' said Ishbel. 'Especially with my feet . . .'

Crog shook his head. 'We await three days and three nights.'

'Why not go now?' asked Wilf.

'Then shall the moon be slender as a sickle.'

Ishbel gave a mocking snort.

Crog looked offended. 'There is sense to this. The moon, she pulls and lets free the tides. When the moon is old and dying, the sea too lies low. That is when the sweet waters of the loch pour down and the tide turns on itself and the waters dance and the wild dogs roar. *That* is when the bowl must go.'

'So just then?' said Ishbel.

'Aye. At that time,' Crog agreed, 'when the water spits and bites and pulls a man down.'

'Oh, it's only a whirlpool, then?' said Wilf.

'No *only*. When you see the dogs . . .' But here Crog waved his hand and his voice trailed away.

'So we put the bowl in this whirlpool and then it disappears God knows where?' Wilf said.

Crog nodded.

'That sounds pretty straightforward,' commented Ishbel. 'We somehow survive for three days. We go there. We chuck the bowl in. We try and set ourselves up with a new life. Remind me – where is it that the Nazi criminals went to? Paraguay? Yeah, we go to Paraguay. We wear little pointy hats and ponchos and live happily ever after.'

'Only . . .'

'Only *what?*' said Ishbel sourly.

'Only the valley men,' replied Crog. 'They will be waiting for us.'

* * *

Crog went down to the woods to set his deer trap. He insisted on going alone, so Wilf and Ishbel remained behind to gather firewood and heap up great prickly bundles of branches and heather in the cave.

When they set off down the mountain, all Wilf could think about was whether Crog had trapped them some breakfast. Even a rat would be good.

They had only just reached the woods when a terrified squeal filled the air. They froze. The scream came again, a high-pitched, wavering treble.

'It's Crog. They must have got him!' hissed Ishbel. They crept in among the pine trees. They were walking on tiptoe, but however careful they were – and the forest floor was soft with pine needles – twigs snapped beneath their feet.

Now there was only a very quiet whimper coming from somewhere up ahead. They inched their way forward.

The whimpering ceased. They pushed on through the undergrowth until the trees opened out into a clearing with a small stream. Wilf passed what he thought was just a hummock; as he did so, Crog stood up and stretched his arms.

'Crog!' exclaimed Wilf. 'You're OK? You gave me such a fright!'

'The good hunter walks the forest silent as smoke,' he said, pursing his lips.

'Sorry, oh silent one.'

'So what *was* that terrible squealing?' asked Ishbel.

'A wounded leveret,' replied Crog.

'A what?' said Wilf.

'It's a posh word for a hare,' Ishbel explained.

'Yummy! Where is it now?'

'*I* was the leveret. It was to bring out the mother.' Crog took a thick wet leaf out of his kaftan pocket and placed it in his mouth. He clenched his hands over his lips and repeated that unbearable squeal.

Wilf covered his ears. 'No wonder they wrung your neck.'

Crog cast him a withering look.

'You still haven't told us what the rope was for,' said Ishbel.

Crog fiddled with the leaf in his hand.

'Did something happen to you?' she persisted. 'Come on, Crog, say something.'

But Crog just scratched at his kaftan and looked away. Finally he said, 'No rabbits. This day we eat tree rats.' He picked up two squashed squirrels by the tail.

'Crog! What did you do? Run them over? They've got blood seeping out of their sides. Yuck,' said Ishbel.

'Stump traps.' Crog shrugged. 'They are always so. But I do not know . . .' He held the squirrels close up to his face and sniffed. 'No sickness, but . . .'

'But *what*?' said Wilf. 'It'll be fine. An adventure. I've never eaten squashed squirrel.'

'Tree rats are russet as the fox,' said Crog, still looking doubtful.

'Don't worry,' said Ishbel. 'They're mostly grey nowadays. The red tree rats are dying out.'

They walked back up to the cave, checking the deer snare and Crog's squirrel trap, which was an old pine stump, with three sticks delicately propping up one end of a felled tree trunk. Under the trunk Crog had placed a piece of wild mushroom as bait.

But this time the bait had been left untouched and there was no third squashed squirrel.

'They learn fast, eh?' said Ishbel.

While Wilf blew on the embers to get the fire going again, Crog skinned and gutted the squirrels using his tusk tool. He then speared the little corpses – without their tails and fur they were very small – and set them over the fire. The squirrels shrank further as they turned from red to pale brown. The eyeballs popped and the little feet curled up horribly. Yet they couldn't wait. They ate the meat half cooked, using some bitter dandelion leaves to eke it out. The tiny morsels of meat tasted delicious.

Afterwards they sat huddled round the fire, pulling the last fragments of meat off the bones, and then cracking them open and sucking out the marrow.

Ishbel looked away as Crog chewed the curled-up feet.

'What do you think? How does it compare with red squirrel?' asked Wilf.

'Bigger,' said Crog, his mouth a mass of little bones. 'But I wish now for the sweet meat of a deer.'

'Don't we all!' exclaimed Ishbel.

There was a pause as Crog crunched on. When he'd swallowed the last few bones, he added, 'We cooked the tree rats in honey.'

'Yeuch,' said Ishbel.

'They were good.' Crog was suddenly talkative. 'All food with honey is good, very good. It keeps too – we buried them. Maybe some remain from my times, still held in their honey.' He pointed to a corner of the cave.

'Per-lease!' said Ishbel.

'For that was my work. I was the honey catcher.'

'Honey catcher? That's not a job!'

'I travelled the woods. I listened with my eyes, and with my nose. I watched the flight of the bees. I used that other sense too. I listened with all of myself – for I had a feeling then for the land and where the hives lay. And most times I was swifter than the bears.'

'Cool!' exclaimed Wilf. 'There were bears then!'

'The honey was so sweet. So very sweet.' Crog gave a little shudder of pleasure.

'But didn't you say you were the bearer of the bowl?' said Ishbel.

'Yes.' Crog shook his head sadly. 'I was that too. I failed afore. I must not fail again.'

'But why did *you* look after the bowl? It was important, wasn't it? And you aren't even a grown-up.'

'I was marked out,' replied Crog, stiffening slightly.

'Are you a king or a priest or something?' asked Wilf. At this, Ishbel raised her eyebrows sceptically.

'No. We were poor,' said Crog. 'My mother was gathering kelp when the pains came upon her. I was born early. Not in water, nor on land, but between the tides. In a place neither of coming nor of going. I did not belong. I was unfinished. Not of this world, nor of the next. So the duty came upon me.' He made an odd clicking noise at the back of his throat and shook his head. Wilf could have sworn his eyes were welling.

Crog moved back, away from the fire. He added, 'I slipped out onto a bed of seaweed.'

Ishbel winced.

'The wind kissed my cheeks, the sand cradled me, the salt water was my coverlet.'

'No wonder you don't seem to mind the cold and wet,' said Wilf. But he thought to himself, *Maybe he smashed his head on the rocks as he came out? That might explain things.*

'My mother . . .' said Crog. 'She wanted this for me. It was her gift to me. It was my blessing . . .'

He paused, took a big breath and gave the fire a prod. 'And it was my curse.'

CHAPTER 16

That night they lay near the fire on their bog-myrtle mattresses which, although scratchy, were at least a little softer than the rocks. Wilf felt safe here, but he knew it was an illusion. If those men came to the mouth of the cave, the only escape was back through the underwater passage.

They only slept in snatches. Mostly they just sat and looked at the flames. Ishbel passed the time by recounting the plots of Hitchcock films, and Wilf reminisced about his own adventures; how he'd bluffed store detectives, and spent a night on the run, hiding curled up in a vat of road salt.

Crog listened to everything, and smiled and scraped away at a bundle of long muddy tendrils he'd grubbed up earlier. Every so often he would pass Wilf and Ishbel little woody plugs of cleaned root. The roots weren't really edible – it was like gnawing on matchsticks. At first Ishbel refused, saying she wasn't a beaver, but later she relented – after all, it gave them something to do. And with no cigarettes to smoke, Wilf was grateful for anything he could chew.

Morning brought clear skies and dry, cold sunshine. From the mouth of the cave they looked out towards the distant coastline, and, down to the south, the metal bridge. There was no sign of *them*.

However, the police hunt was still on. Throughout the morning they heard helicopters on the far side of the ridge. And when they climbed back up the mountain-side and looked down into the valley where they had abandoned the car, they saw flashing blue lights.

At least down in the woods they couldn't be seen. And it was here that they spent the morning. They checked the stump traps, but there were no squirrels. The deer noose had somehow got dislodged; Crog looked worried when he saw this. He reset the snare and they walked on down through the trees until they reached the clearing with the river. Here they washed and stretched out on the bracken, trying to soak up a little of the chilly sunshine. But it was hard to relax. Wilf was always watching, always starting at the slightest sound. He thought he saw some-thing move behind the trees – a sudden thickening of the undergrowth, a flicker of shadows.

They spoke in hushed voices. Ishbel didn't believe *they* would just wait quietly down at the bridge. The men – or 'gougers', as she called them – were clever with technology. She thought they might be using spy drones, those little remote-control aircraft that the American military were operating in the Middle East.

Crog looked flummoxed by this. So Ishbel tried to explain who the Americans were and what the wars in the Middle East were all about and how drones worked. None of this made any sense to Crog, so she told him what a country was and why religions were different. But he looked more and more baffled, and in the end she lost patience. 'Never mind,' she said. 'It doesn't matter!' And she closed her eyes and let out a long tired sigh.

Crog turned to Wilf.

'Put it this way,' said Wilf. 'Drones are . . . Well, they're sort of like little metal fairies.'

Crog nodded and seemed happy with this. But a little later Wilf caught him looking at them both quite oddly.

Wilf didn't scan the sky for drones, but he understood Ishbel's unease. There was something strange and unsettling about this quiet time. They needed to rest after their escape from London and the terrible march over the mountains, but somehow this little interlude didn't feel right.

If their enemies caught up with them now, where would they go? Was this a trap? Was a noose tightening around them? What were they doing to protect themselves? They were doing nothing – just waiting. Of course, they *had* to wait: according to Crog's reading of the night sky, there were still three days until the moon would be right and the tides ready. But Wilf had a creeping sense of dread. He knew they were waiting, but he didn't think it was for the moon or the tides. Instead they were waiting for something unknown. Something worse.

And Wilf was right.

If only they'd been less tired, they might have picked up the signs. Wilf had smelled a chemical tang in the morning air, but he had thought no more of it. And he and Ishbel had ignored Crog's worried face when he discovered the dislodged deer snare. Crog had become even quieter. Now, while Wilf and Ishbel sunned themselves by the stream, Crog sat on his haunches, his hands completely still.

After a while Wilf felt his bowels grumble – last night's squirrel had loosened him up inside. He got to his feet and quickly made for the trees. He needed a bit of distance – he knew the sounds from his guts would be explosive.

When he came to the edge of the trees, he gathered some large dock leaves to wipe himself and crouched down behind a clump of gorse.

He had picked a good perch for his business. If he craned his neck, there was a view of the grassland below and a sheep trail that led past the gorse and on up the mountainside. He really was in the wilds. He took a deep breath. Again there was that same chemical smell he'd noted earlier. Only this time it was much stronger.

He closed his eyes and inhaled thoughtfully. Service station forecourt . . . Definitely petrol. And now there was a murmur of voices too. They were quite faint, but something told him that this was no trick of the mind. They had real substance and did not come from inside his head. There were people out there. He peered through the gorse. For a moment he saw nothing. Then, on the shoulder of the mountainside, two shadows emerged. A second later the men came into view: Badger and Snout were coming his way.

Wilf froze. They'd hear him if he moved now. He shrank back – hunkered down, quietened his breathing, and prayed to be flat and low as a stone. If only the gorse were thicker. His bowels gave another gripe. He clenched his muscles. Any sound now would kill him. And the smell might give him away.

The men were carrying some fancy-looking equipment. Each had a large red canister – like a giant jerry can – strapped to his back. The canisters were connected to steel hose attachments and they were spraying the ground as they went.

They were coming towards him. Wilf looked away. It was too scary to watch and he didn't want them getting that eyes-on-the-back-of-the-neck feeling. If they ever had any feelings.

Snout and Badger were coming closer. He could hear their footsteps. He just wanted it to be over quickly. But what a way to be found! Crouching with his jeans around his ankles, his own mire under him. How humiliating was that!

The men were talking quietly. Wilf could feel cramp building up in his thighs, but he ignored it and strained his ears. What were they saying? It wasn't English, yet it wasn't completely foreign, either: sounds and words of which, at any moment, he felt he could catch the meaning. Only he didn't. It was oddly familiar – a language he felt he ought to know.

Suddenly there was silence. The men had stopped talking. Maybe they had seen something? Or smelled something? Wilf could hear their footsteps only a couple of metres away.

They were passing his gorse bush. Then Badger's coat brushed against it and he stopped.

Wilf shut his eyes – he completely sympathized with

ostriches now: if only he could sink his head in the ground. The smell of petrol was very strong and he could hear the hiss of a hose.

One of the men – probably Badger – muttered something in an exasperated voice. Wilf opened his eyes just a fraction, and through the branches he saw their legs – they were still in those city suits. Badger was removing a piece of gorse that had caught on his coat. He released the thorns, brushed down his coat, and they walked on up the mountainside.

Wilf crouched there, his thighs shaking; the petrol fumes gathered painfully in his throat. Why petrol? It was obvious. There was only one reason to douse a mountainside in petrol.

How long had they got?

Wilf strained his ears. When he could no longer hear the men, he pulled up his trousers and darted back through the trees.

When he got to the river, Crog was on his feet. Ishbel was doing up her boots.

'They're here! Let's go!' hissed Wilf.

'The valley men? They saw us?' asked Crog.

'They're about to burn us out!'

'A coward's way,' said Crog sneeringly.

'Come on! We have to go!'

Behind him Wilf heard crackling. A line of bright flames shot along the ground towards them as if a furnace were roaring under the ground and coming up through every gap it could find. When the fire reached Wilf's feet – and this happened so fast he couldn't quite take it in – a great lick of flame burst up in front of him, and he fell backwards. He quickly got to his feet and made for the stream.

'Run!' shouted Ishbel.

The only possible route was along the river, Wilf thought: all around them the undergrowth was on fire – the men had been very generous with the petrol. Now, faster and faster, the heat stoked the flames, and there were great muffled roars as entire trees suddenly caught and burned upwards in one stroke.

Ishbel and Crog were already running downstream – though the woods were thicker here, the fire denser and the air more full of smoke. That couldn't be right. But *they* were up the mountain, weren't they?

Wilf followed. The river was narrow and the stones slippery. He had to bend almost double to avoid the burning branches that flicked back at him after Ishbel and Crog had pushed their way through. If they didn't get out soon, they'd suffocate. Wasn't that how people usually died in fires? Wilf kept going, but the air was growing hotter and the fire was gathering apace.

More and more frequently came the *whumph!* of a tree exploding into flames. And there was another sound too – the sharp crack of gunfire up on the hillside. Later Wilf would wonder how the men could aim through all the smoke and fire, but not now. Now he smelled burning flesh and hair. The poor squirrels and voles must be dying all around him. Yet, as he ran on, the scorching smell stayed with him. The side of his neck felt hot – it was his own hair on fire. Wilf splashed on down the river, and as he ran, he slapped frantically at the smouldering patches on his head. He tried to think. Where could they go? He pushed his way through another mass of burning branches, and saw that at last the trees were thinning out. Soon he was out of the wood, the fire mostly behind him. He followed the stream into a narrow rocky crevice.

Ahead of him he'd seen Crog leaping nimbly from boulder to boulder. But now Crog had disappeared. And where was Ishbel? The river was flattening out now and he could see some way downstream. But there was no sign of them.

And then, beside a little waterfall, Wilf saw the still figure of Ishbel; she was just lying there, only her head and shoulders out of the water; her face was very white. Crog was crouching down beside her. There was no blood this

CHAPTER 17

Ishbel groaned.

'Ishie!' exclaimed Wilf. Relief surged through him. Then rage. He turned on Crog. 'You said she was dead! All she's done is knock herself out!'

'Her spirit travelled,' said Crog calmly. 'Now it returns.'

She moaned again. They heaved her out onto the bank and propped her up against a rock, hidden from the mountainside. Water sluiced off her clothes.

'We've got to get her moving!' said Wilf. 'Ishie!' He slapped her cheeks. She didn't respond. He slapped her again and shook her shoulders. 'Wake up, Ishie! Wake up! We can't hang around here!'

Ishbel moved her head away, and again she groaned.

'She returns,' said Crog.

'Yeah, but how would you like it if I said your sister was dead when she wasn't?' Wilf gave Ishbel a couple more angry slaps. She jerked her head back and opened her eyes with a startled expression.

'Never had a sister, never had a brother,' said Crog

dolefully. 'I was alone in the world. I was my own sun, my own stars, my own moon.'

Ishbel clasped her head for a moment. 'Wilf,' she said. 'Do me a favour. Slap *him* instead.'

Wilf looked back up the mountain. The fire was still spreading above them, the trees aflame, the gorse spitting and crackling. In places the ground itself seemed to be smouldering, sending up columns of thick smoke that billowed out across the slope. The heat made Wilf's face flush; Ishbel's clothes steamed.

There was no sign of the men, but they couldn't be far away.

'The smoke is our friend,' said Crog.

'Precisely,' said Wilf. 'Let's get out of here before it clears.'

They helped Ishbel to her feet. She'd hurt her shoulder in the fall, and twisted an ankle: she winced the moment she put any weight on it. 'My head feels like it's been slammed between two dustbin lids,' she moaned. But then she seemed to brace herself. She turned to Crog and said, 'Where will they not find us? Where can we go now?'

Crog pointed northwest.

They clambered up the far side of the gully and, when they reached the flank of the mountainside, took a track heading north. Crog was in the lead, running nimbly,

Ishbel hobbling after him, her clothes still heavy with water. Wilf brought up the rear, bent over – he would be the nearest target if the shooting began again.

On the brow of the hill, Crog stopped abruptly. Ishbel and Wilf joined him – and for a moment they crouched in the heather and looked down. In front of them lay another, much smaller valley – a sudden fold in the land; pine plantations covered the upper reaches, while below, grasslands dotted with gorse and rhododendron led down to the sea. On the far side of the bay they saw a line of cliffs that ringed the way north; at the foot of the valley, behind a ridge of trees, Wilf could make out a small scoop of beach with a jetty.

Ishbel was shivering violently.

'Let's get out of the wind,' he said, pulling her arm.

They ran on over the brow and down the slope until they reached the wood. After pushing their way through the trees, they came out on a track that zigzagged down the mountain. They followed this, even though it was risky – anyone could come round a corner and see them. But they had to put some distance between themselves and the men, and Wilf knew they wouldn't be far behind. So they ran on and on down the zigzags, stopping only occasionally to catch their breath. And all the time

Wilf thought, *We are running away. But where are we running to? What lies ahead?*

They reached the tarmacked road at the bottom, dashed across and then ran through a hummocky field. When they reached a stand of Scots pines, they crouched down in a shallow hollow between two trees.

'There must be somewhere better we can hide.' Wilf scanned the valley.

A minute ago the forest above them had been green and clear, but now a line of fire was raking across the mountainside. Where could they go? To the north, the cliffs barricaded their escape. The valley was a cul-de-sac.

'Fire and stone withset us,' murmured Crog. Suddenly he swivelled his head round and pointed south. 'We go!' he said.

Wilf followed Crog's finger. At first he saw nothing – just the road they had crossed, which followed the contours of the mountain and disappeared round the coast. Then he heard the car engine . . . and before he had time to think, he saw a silver car. It turned into their valley.

They all shrank back, flattening themselves into the dip in the land. Wilf didn't dare look out. He heard the car stop. One door slammed shut, then another. He peered out – it had stopped at the narrowest point in the valley and the men had separated. Badger was skirting the edge of the woods, Snout was on their side of the road, searching in the scrubland. The men were clearly going to comb the valley from south to north. *They're pros*, thought Wilf miserably.

'Got any more caves?' hissed Ishbel.

Crog shook his head.

'Our only chance, then, is the jetty,' said Ishbel. 'Someone might have a boat.'

The jetty was only 200 metres away. They waited until Snout had disappeared into an avenue of rhododendron bushes, and then ran, crouching low, darting from rhododendron to rhododendron, checking all the while on where Snout was. Wilf was waiting for the sound of gunfire – Snout might have an excellent vantage point.

When they reached the shore, they hid behind some rocks and took stock.

Luckily, someone *had* left a boat beside the jetty. It was a sturdy wooden rowing boat, wide-bellied and low in the water. The hull was heaped with floats and nets and buckets.

Wilf peered out – no sign of Snout.

'We wait,' said Crog. 'We attend for the cloak of night.'

Ishbel looked at him disbelievingly.

'He's right,' said Wilf. 'Otherwise they'll pick us off on the open sea.'

'But what do we do in the meantime?' asked Ishbel.

Crog jerked his head in the direction of the jetty.

'Under there?' She gave him a look.

'If we get right underneath, close to the rock face, they might not see us,' said Wilf, only half believing it.

The jetty was supported by a network of crisscrossing wooden beams. Wilf and Ishbel – Crog was doing something by the boat and was some way behind them – hoisted themselves up and climbed from strut to slimy strut until they came to the narrow dark space directly underneath the walkway, where it joined the rock face.

Wilf listened. No footsteps. 'All we have to do is wait,' he whispered.

'And pray,' added Ishbel.

After a while Crog joined them. He was carrying a small pail.

'What's that?' whispered Wilf.

'Good,' said Crog, chewing. He offered up the pail and Wilf looked in. Small pale things glistened and wriggled.

'Sorry, Crog. I don't eat food that crawls. Nor does Ishie.'

Crog shrugged, thrust his hand back in the pail and then spilled some of the contents into his mouth.

'What's he got there?' asked Ishbel.

'Bait. Probably maggots.' Wilf wished Crog wasn't quite so close to him. 'Where did you get it, Crog?'

But Crog was chewing.

'He'll have got it from the boat,' said Ishbel. 'At least it means it's used regularly.'

'Ssssssh,' hissed Crog.

They waited in silence.

Wilf could hear only his own heartbeat and the slap of the tide. Then, very faintly, far away, he heard footsteps on the shore. They became louder, gathering pace. Wilf was sure it was Snout, for Badger had been up by the woods. Had he seen them? He was only metres away now.

Wilf shut his eyes. There was absolutely nothing he could do. He just had to wait as the steps came nearer.

He concentrated on breathing. He told himself to just blow out little puffs of air and hope to survive. When Snout was almost close enough to be breathing the same air, he changed direction and headed along beside the jetty towards the sea. A minute later he was back, shoes clumping overhead, making the struts creak. He walked down the jetty, paused and then strode back up again. Gradually the footsteps receded.

Finally Wilf opened his eyes again. Crog was making his way through the last of the maggots, upending the pail over his mouth and scraping out the inside with his hand.

'He missed the bowl,' he whispered between mouthfuls.

'What do you mean?'

'He did not *feel* the bowl. I foresaw his coming and cast it into the water.'

'What? You've got rid of it? Already?' exclaimed Wilf.

'Nay. It lies in its casket, and the casket is tied under the boat,' said Crog. 'But through the water he felt it not.'

'So *now* you tell us that the aluminium foil wasn't enough and that they've still got some weird psychic connection thing,' said Ishbel. 'So whatever happens they'll find us. Thanks, Crog. That's good news.'

'Underwater and bound in metal, they can barely sense the bowl. The hog-faced man may have felt something – he went hard by the boat. But he is waylaid. He is dulled by having your' – here Crog waved a dismissive hand – 'your quick new tools. Now he does not trust his senses.'

'You quite like a few quick new tools too,' said Ishbel. 'You're a right one for a flushing toilet.'

Crog didn't deign to reply.

The rest of the afternoon passed very slowly. Wilf soon discovered that there was no possible way to get comfortable. If he crouched down, his legs ached, and if he sat on the cross beams, they dug into his bottom. Ishbel, who had never got properly dry after her fall, complained of the cold. Meanwhile Crog sat with a reptilian stillness. Every so often he picked a stray maggot off his rope, but otherwise he didn't move at all. Wilf wondered if this was how he'd passed all those centuries in the dark: staying very still, his hand darting out every so often to catch a passing insect.

Finally, after what seemed like an eternity, night fell and they crawled out from under the jetty. While Wilf and Ishbel shook the pins and needles from their limbs, Crog retrieved the soaking box with the bowl. Then they all scrambled into the boat.

Wilf and Ishbel each took an oar and they rowed together, keeping a steady rhythm. Every time they pulled back on the oars, the little boat rocked and the waves slapped against the side. The mountainside was now scattered with tiny orange glow worms where the undergrowth still smouldered.

Slowly, so slowly, the boat pulled out into the bay. The waves were bigger now, and it had started to rain big soft raindrops. The valley was receding into the distance; there was just a faint white path of moonlight and the glitter of the oars striking the water. What lay beyond, Wilf didn't know. Some terrible Scottish island with nothing but cliffs and gannets? Or were they heading directly out into the ocean?

If only he had a map. Or Ishbel had her mobile. But instead their direction finder was Crog, sitting in the stern with his hands round Gordon's box, looking out to sea.

'Are we going to row all night?' asked Ishbel, pausing to stretch and pull the sleeves of her oilskin over her palms. Wilf put his oar down and blew into his hands. He couldn't see, but he knew he'd rubbed the skin raw. There was no point in saying anything, though – Crog might volunteer more urine.

'OK, Ishie,' he said, trying to forget his hands. 'Back to it.'

They rowed on. The tiny slice of moon was behind a bank of cloud now, so it seemed to Wilf as if they were rowing into pure darkness and there was nothing now but the wind and the open water. He sensed that the waves were getting higher, beginning to spill over the sides of the boat. Soon they'd have to start bailing.

Crog didn't offer to row. He just sat crouched there, making faint clicking noises. Every so often he would gesture with his head – indicating that the boat should go a little more to the right, or to the left. He seemed so confident, but what did he know?

'Where are we going?' asked Wilf. 'Where are you taking us?'

'It's the water. The water that carries us,' replied Crog.

'Funny, that. Feels to me like *we're* the ones doing the work,' said Ishbel. She yanked crossly on her oar.

Crog's clicking sounds grew louder.

'And what's that over there?' Ishbel pointed into the night.

Wilf followed her gaze. A little over to one side the darkness seemed somehow thicker, as if something huge was towering up out of the water. 'What do you think it is?'

'A kraken probably,' she replied. 'That's the one thing missing from our Wonderful Scottish Experience.'

'It is rock, just rock,' said Crog quietly. 'But we come to the shore soon.'

'How do you know, Crog? It's pitch-dark here. I don't see any night-vision goggles on you,' said Ishbel.

'Open your ears . . . You can hear the shore.'

Wilf shut his eyes and tried to listen. He certainly couldn't hear the shore. The rain had stopped now and there was no sound except the oars plashing through the water, and the sigh of the wind and the occasional *click, click, click* from Crog. Wilf sank back into the rhythm of rowing, mindlessly leaning forward and back. The boat slid on into the darkness.

After a while Ishbel said, 'Crog, why do you keep making that clicking noise?'

'So I may hear better,' he replied.

'Oh! I see. You're echolocating. You really *are* a bat! That explains everything.'

Wilf and Ishbel laughed, and even Crog emitted a rusty little croak. And it seemed to Wilf that in that moment of companionship, all the terror and danger and discomfort of the day melted away.

Then Crog said, 'Soon we reach land. There will be sweet water and good things to eat: mushrooms, fish, mice.'

And the boat scraped the sea bed and juddered to a halt. They had arrived.

CHAPTER 18

Fumbling in the dark, their feet slipping on the seaweed, they pulled the boat up onto the beach and moored it to a large rock.

Wilf walked with his hands held out in front. Crog didn't have to feel his way; he went on ahead and then called to the others. He had found a washed-up tree trunk that they could sit on. It was lying beneath a sand bank in the lee of the wind.

They huddled together, waiting for the dawn. Crog snored gently, and Wilf watched in the darkness for lights – the men would surely have lights, however techie they were.

Ishbel leaned her head on his shoulder. Her clothes were still damp and she was shivering. 'I don't think I'll *ever* be warm again.'

They sat listening to the waves and the wind and Crog's snores. Wilf thought, *Any moment now, just when I'm beginning to get drowsy, THEY will come up behind us. Or an arc light will scan the beach, pin us to the log and shoot us.*

He stared into the darkness, but there was nothing.

Ishbel lay down with her head on his lap and he did his best to cover her body with his jacket. Slowly, as dawn came upon them, the sea emerged out of the darkness. In front of them was an expanse of still water, and beyond this, an outline of hills, so far away that Wilf thought they might be part of Ireland. Nearer, towards the middle of the bay, he saw a small rocky island, with the crumbling remains of a castle perched on the top.

Wilf gave Ishbel's shoulder a squeeze. 'Look! There's an island with a castle.'

Ishbel didn't sit up, but murmured, 'Looks familiar. I've seen it somewhere before.'

'That's what we passed in the night,' said Wilf. 'That was your kraken.'

She didn't reply.

'Do you think the men have given up? Perhaps they're not hunting us any longer.'

Crog, who Wilf had thought was asleep, gave out a long, tired sigh.

'What's that supposed to mean?'

'The sea and the rivers will run dry afore they lay down their arms,' said Crog.

Wilf glanced round once more just to check that the men

weren't coming up from behind. Now that the darkness had lifted, he saw, a little way from the beach, a large white house set among trees. It was a long sprawling building facing out to sea, its walls covered in ivy. There was a field separating the house and its grounds from the beach.

'Hey! Look!' Wilf nudged Ishbel.

She turned and gave a startled gasp, then got to her feet, holding his shoulder for balance. She was staring at the house. 'It's all shuttered up! It's so much smaller than I remember.'

Wilf looked at her, bemused. 'What's up?' he said. 'Has the cold got to you?'

'Look at the house!'

'Er, I *am* looking at the house. And what?' Wilf was conscious of Crog watching them both carefully.

'You don't get it, do you?' said Ishbel.

'What am I supposed to get?' Why, he wondered, was she always wrong-footing him?

'This is Mum's old house. We're home.'

'What!' said Wilf. This couldn't be right. He looked again at the house, hoping that something – anything – would strike a chord. If this really *had* been his old house, he should be feeling something, shouldn't he? He should be all gaspy and astonished like Ishbel. But instead he just felt uncomfortable. His mind was dead. His memories were so hazy they were nothing really. He thought, *Your childhood is part of who you are. But there's nothing here for me*.

'It *is*. I'm certain,' said Ishbel. 'It's Mum's old house. I know this is weird, but it's definitely the place. We used to come here on holiday all the time. We used to play in that field there. Don't you remember?'

'Are you *sure*?' asked Wilf.

'Certain! I remember clearly. I could draw you a plan of everything. All the little service rooms downstairs – and upstairs there's that long corridor with our night nursery at the end.'

'A *night nursery!* This is the twenty-first century, Ishbel,' said Wilf.

'Things were different up here.'

'I don't remember any *night nursery*,' persisted Wilf.

'But you don't remember *anything*! Honestly, Wilf, what have you been taking? Keep off the glue. It goes through your mind like drain cleaner. There won't be anything left of you at this rate.'

'I don't do glue,' said Wilf primly. 'Not after Denzil.'

A vague recollection of sitting on a staircase at night when he should have been in bed came back to him.

'Was there a staircase with funny spirally bits on the banisters?' he asked.

'Barley-twist spindles? Yup.' Ishbel sucked her teeth

and added, 'I don't know how you can forget so much. But I suppose girls are just more advanced, aren't they?'

'Now who needs slapping?'

They walked through the field and up to the house. Ishbel said her legs felt funny and leaned on Wilf's arm. When they reached the big double doors facing the sea, she sat on the steps with Crog. Wilf investigated the lock, but it was very sturdy, with metal bolts holding the frame in place. So they made their way down some steps at the side and round to the back, where he kicked open a dusty little door, which according to Ishbel would lead to the buttery.

As Wilf tumbled inside, something flew into his face. He ducked and crouched on the floor with his arms over his head.

Bats – the air was alive with them. His eyes weren't used to the darkness, so he had no idea – was it just a few? No, far more. Maybe ten . . . maybe a hundred, all wheeling around. There was *nothing* in the world – almost – that Wilf hated more. Spiders OK. Snakes not great. But bats? There wasn't a word in the language for the way they made him feel. Those hateful little faces.

He was still on the floor with his hands over his head when the bats, in a rush of black wind, flew out of the door.

Ishbel came in and pulled back the shutters. Light spilled in, and now Wilf could see the room clearly: the stone floor, the long stone shelves and basins. Everywhere was covered in small black bat droppings.

'Are you sure this is Mum's old house?' he asked.

'Absolutely,' replied Ishbel, rubbing her arms to get warm. She pointed to a barrel on a stand; it was swathed in cobwebs.

'That's the old churn,' she said. 'You turn the handle and after absolutely ages the milk turns into a lump of butter and goes *thump, thump, thump*. Don't you remember?'

'Wouldn't fancy any butter from that.' Wilf grimaced.

He went over to the door on the far side of the room and pressed the latch. What did it lead to? He had no idea. But he thought, *I am entering my memories. I am entering my own past.*

The hinges moved stickily, and the door opened to reveal a wide stoneflagged hallway lit by skylights. 'The servants' quarters,' whispered Ishbel. She pointed to each door leading off the hallway. 'Larder, second larder, cleaning cupboard, coal store, gun room – never went in there, it was always locked – drying room, ironing room. Don't you remember?'

Wilf shook his head.

Ishbel pushed a couple of the doors open. 'They had rooms here you'd never dream of having nowadays.'

'And they'll all be full of bat turds,' he said. 'And there's nothing to eat in any of them.'

'Exactly.'

Wilf led the way up a narrow flight of stairs and into a large, low-ceilinged kitchen that smelled powerfully of mice. Crog pulled at the old fridge door; the seal sucked open, the dark inside breathed rot. If only someone were living here, Wilf thought, then at least there would be some food. He tried the light switches, but nothing happened. He opened a drawer of tarnished silver cutlery, then picked up a spoon and rubbed the end – there was his family crest: the little oak tree and the sword. So Ishbel was right – it was their home.

'Ishie, this is not right,' he said. 'This house is like it is because we've got too much money. Normal people can't afford to keep extra homes everywhere. And if they do have an empty house, they let it. Or they sell it. Dad does neither. He just leaves everything to rot.'

But Ishbel wasn't listening. 'Ahh!' she cried, approaching a cobwebby dresser as if it were an old friend. She picked up a small wooden box and rattled it. 'You know what'll be in here, don't you . . .? Don't you remember?'

'I wish you'd stop saying *Don't you remember*,' muttered Wilf.

'Well, I'll tell you: a couple of bobbins, a brocade purse, a stone apple with a little chip on the side, and a felt mouse in a ballroom dress.'

She opened the lid. Two bobbins, a purse, a fake apple – even the tired-looking felt mouse – were all there.

'Don't you remember?' Ishbel beamed. 'Wilf, you *must* remember the mouse.'

'No.' He wished she would talk about something else. Even climate change. Or the European Union. Anything.

'And the mysterious gun room with the locked door?' she went on. 'D'you remember that?'

'No. But I do remember the cabinet with the Tibetan knuckledusters.'

'That's strange.' Ishbel frowned. 'I've got an excellent memory, but I don't recall any knuckledusters. Do you *really* remember that?'

'Of course I don't!' said Wilf wearily. 'You know me. I don't remember anything.'

'But there must be something. You *must* remember Mum . . .' said Ishbel.

He certainly remembered her body. The undertakers had put her in a backlit display unit with a little curtain and a glass front – as if she were a snake in a reptile house.

And when they drew back the curtain, there she'd been. Still as a snake, and with one eye ever so slightly open, so you could just see a little slit of white. And he had wondered then, just as he wondered now: *What do the dead see?*

But he cast that thought aside and shut his eyes. He was back in his mother's house, where he'd spent his early years, but nothing seemed familiar. His past was a locked box – the one thing he couldn't break and enter. Only the barest memories stirred in a faraway part of his mind.

'She had freckles on her arms, didn't she?' he checked.

Ishbel snorted. 'Freckles? And that's all you remember?'

They went through the kitchen and into a grand dining room spread with dustsheets, giant patches of damp erupting across the ceiling. This room led to a central hallway, where Wilf felt cheered by the sight of the twisted banister spindles.

'Let's go up,' he said.

Just as Ishbel had predicted, the first-floor landing was a long corridor with doors leading off on either side.

'So where's this night nursery?' asked Wilf.

'Door at the end.' Ishbel had sat down halfway up the stairs. 'I'm not feeling too good. Get us a blanket while you're up there.'

Wilf hurried along the corridor. If anything brought his childhood back to him, this surely would. There was no point delaying, no point getting nervous. He should just go into the room without thinking about it too much.

He turned the doorknob, but the door was jammed in the frame. He pushed and pushed again. He pushed a third time. Finally it sprang open.

Wilf clutched the frame and stepped back just in time. In front of him was a three-metre drop. The nursery floor had collapsed! He looked down on a sea of rubble and broken bedsteads, and laughed with relief.

He called to Ishbel to come and see, but there was no reply. When he came back down the stairs, she was still sitting huddled and shivering on the step. He went back upstairs and, in a chest on the landing, found a moth-eaten quilt. He brought it down and put it round her.

Ishbel didn't react.

'Are you OK?' he asked.

'Yeah, whatever. It's just the cold's got to me. Where's Crog?'

'He'll be looking for food,' said Wilf. 'I'll go and find him.'

He found Crog bent double in the laundry room, spitting onto the floor.

Wilf looked at him – his face was all puckered up. Then he cast his eyes around the room and noticed a metal cabinet with the door wrenched open. On a shelf inside were tea bags, some hardened sugar, a can of condensed milk, some solidified Nescafé and two packets of powdered oxtail soup. And spilled across the floor were hundreds of tiny saccharine tablets.

'You thought they were sweets, didn't you?' said Wilf. 'You thought they'd be like the fudge?'

Crog, still spitting, nodded miserably.

They searched for food in the rest of the servants' quarters but there was little else. On a rack in the larder Crog found a plait of ancient onions. He picked up a shrivelled bulb by its brown stalk and sniffed it thoughtfully.

'No,' said Wilf. 'That's not edible. Not now. It's more like a shrunken head of some weird alien.'

There was also a shelf of tins. They were mostly rusted through at the bottom, but there were a couple of cans of baked beans that seemed OK. Wilf found a can opener and opened one – the colour had leached out of the tomato sauce and the beans were translucent with age.

He inspected the contents warily. 'Alien's eggs. They hatch into those shrunken brown things.'

Crog looked startled.

'I was only joking,' said Wilf.

Crog dabbed a finger in the sauce and licked it. 'Old,' he said.

'So are you,' replied Wilf.

Crog smiled at him tiredly.

Back in the hall, they saw that Ishbel was still on the step. Only she was no longer sitting upright. She'd slumped onto the stairs as if she'd landed there from a great height.

Wilf ran up to her. 'What's the matter, Ishie?' he asked. Her eyes were closed, her face was white and her mouth lolled open. He shook her shoulder and she barely moaned.

Crog said, 'I light her a fire.'

But now Ishbel was no longer even shivering. Wilf tried lifting her onto her feet, but her legs buckled immediately. So he picked her up as if she were a sleeping child and carried her into the book-lined study, where Crog was lighting a fire.

It was a corner room, with windows looking both straight out over the bay and to the woods at the side. There was a second door leading directly outside. Wilf noted this; the door would be useful if they had to escape. *When* they had to escape.

Crog fed the fire another crumpled book.

Wilf eased Ishbel's body onto the hearth rug and then ran upstairs to the chest and quickly pulled out some blankets and more quilts. He brought them down, laid a blanket on the rug, and placed several quilts on top. He pulled off Ishbel's wet boots, then her jeans, coat and top. She drowsily half helped him while Crog stared at her limp white body.

'It's called a bra!' said Wilf. 'They all have them. Please don't give me that ghost-ate-my-breakfast look.'

Crog blushed. Wilf thought he looked very different with apple-red cheeks – almost healthy.

Wilf tucked Ishbel under the quilts, and he and Crog ate the baked beans straight from the tins. They didn't taste great, but after the food in the cave – all those gristly little bits of squirrel and the stringy roots and the dandelion leaves – this was soft and easy to eat. Wilf tried to spoon some beans into Ishbel's mouth, but she turned her head away.

'Food. Water,' said Crog. 'We must go agathering.' He pointed to two pails he'd brought from the kitchen.

'You think of nothing else,' said Wilf. 'Just food and more food and that bowl. You're a one-track CD.'

'A CD?' Crog looked puzzled.

'Never mind.'

They waited until Ishbel was soundly asleep, then Wilf

undid the bolts on the side door, letting in a gust of damp morning air. Pails in hand, they went out.

Wilf and Crog spent most of the day foraging, with Wilf returning to the house every so often to feed the fire with the wood they'd collected and see to Ishbel. She didn't wake up, and seemed to be feverish now. Each time he came back, her brow was a little hotter. What could he do? He tried spooning water into her mouth, but she kept turning away. And yet she was so restless – her body lying at awkward angles, as if she couldn't get comfortable. All the while her mouth was open, dribbling a blackish liquid onto the blanket.

Down on the beach, Crog was a food-finding dynamo. Wilf looked up every so often to check the sea and the sky for signs of the men, but Crog was intent on gathering food; having cleared the shore of mussels, he thrust his hands into rock pools and scooped out handfuls of sea anemones. He grabbed speedy little crabs, and flattened them against his palm. He flicked limpets off their rocks and combed the wet sand for cockles. Wilf was put to shame: his harvest was a fraction of Crog's and his hands were clumsy with cold and soon covered in cuts.

In the afternoon they went further afield, deep

into the birch woods. Here they gathered tiny poisonous-looking orange mushrooms growing in the leaf mould, and filled their buckets with icy water from the stream. As the light began to dim, they headed back home.

Some time had passed since Wilf's last visit to the house, and when he opened the study door, the air seemed still and muggy. For one terrible moment he thought they'd been away too long. Had Ishbel died? Had the men been and gone?

But then he heard the rattly breathing. Ishbel was still asleep, hair sticking to her face. The black liquid dribbling from her mouth had formed a gummy little pool on the blanket.

They crouched down beside her, and Wilf noticed a throbbing vein on the side of her forehead. Crog shook Ishbel's shoulder but she didn't wake. He took her head in both hands and turned her face towards him. Her mouth dropped open and he lifted her lower lip and looked at her gums.

Crog dipped his forefinger in the black dribble, sniffed at the finger, then gave it a lick. Wilf watched, appalled, but Crog didn't notice; he was looking up at the corner of the room, concentrating on the taste. Then he shook his head.

'Well?' said Wilf. 'What's up?'

Crog shook his head again.

'What's that supposed to mean?'

'Black wind,' said Crog. 'Bile in the belly. Bad.'

'How bad?'

Crog shrugged. 'In the reaches of the night she will pass beyond.'

'I wish you'd speak English,' said Wilf. 'What are you gabbling about?'

'Pass to the world of the spirits,' said Crog. Then he added, 'And stay there.'

'What? She's going to die?' Wilf's voice was squeaky with emotion.

'There are many there. She will not be alone.'

'No, she certainly won't! Not with you licking her spit,' said Wilf.

Crog blinked reproachfully at him.

Wilf looked away, then sat up straighter and said, 'We need an ambulance!'

Crog's brow furrowed. 'That word is new to me.'

'We've got to get her to hospital,' cried Wilf.

But he knew how hollow this sounded. There was no road near the house. There was no telephone. To get back into that little boat with Ishbel so ill would be impossible. And he was sure that it was the journey here, rowing through the night in those wet clothes, that had made her ill in the first place.

'Ishie!' Wilf gave her a shake. 'Ishie!' He spoke loudly in her ear, but she didn't respond. Her skin felt so hot and damp.

He had to do *something*.

'Water!' he cried.

Crog brought over one of the pails, and Wilf propped Ishbel's head up on his lap. He took a ladleful of water and tried to tip it into her mouth. But just as it reached her lips, her head turned away. He tried again, and the water slopped down her chin. He dipped the corner of a blanket in the pail and tried to squeeze the water into her mouth. Again her head moved away.

'Leave her,' said Crog.

'She's sweating like a pig,' said Wilf. 'She'll dehydrate.'

'If we force water into her, she will drown in her dreams.'

'I don't know what you're talking about,' Wilf said angrily. But he gave up with the water and gently laid Ishbel's hot head back on the blanket. What more could he do for her? He pulled the cover off a cushion, dipped it in the water and placed it on her forehead.

That night Wilf and Crog didn't sleep. They sat by the fire

and boiled up the limpets and cockles and mussels in a small saucepan. The box stood out of the way on the mantelpiece, and between them lay Ishbel. As the night went on, she became more agitated. She called out. She fought the quilts. She moaned. At one point she sat up with her eyes wide open, and held her arms out to something or somebody that she saw in front of her. Her words were muffled, but she seemed to be pleading. Wilf couldn't understand what she was saying . . . something about flying birds?

'It's all right, Ishie.' He shuffled closer and tried to comfort her. Ishbel ignored him. Then, suddenly, she gave a little whimper, shut her eyes and slumped back down again.

Wilf lifted the cushion cover and felt her brow. Hot. But she was still breathing.

'This night is a long black road,' said Crog tiredly.

Wilf didn't reply.

'Full of ravines and storms and black water,' added Crog.

'Yeah,' said Wilf, 'but there are service stations too. Here, have a limpet.'

He passed the saucepan to Crog, who took a limpet and prised it out of its shell. The limpets were really just cold, rubberized sea water, but it was something to do.

There was a companionable silence as they both chewed.

Eventually Wilf said, 'Crog, were you ever ill?'

'I suffered,' he replied cryptically.

'Suffered from what?'

'The milky flux.'

'That sounds disgusting,' said Wilf.

'I had bules too, and cankers.' Crog was warming to the subject. 'And dropsy pulled me down in the long winter nights.'

'Oh,' said Wilf. He gave the fire another poke.

Ishbel called out again during the night, but in the early hours of the morning, her illness took another worrying turn. She lay very still, her lips bluish and her face pale, as if all the heat and vigour had been drained out of her. She was still breathing, but only very faintly.

'It's like she's closing down,' said Wilf, leaning over Ishbel for the umpteenth time. He wanted to cry.

'I'd feel better if she moaned at least,' he went on. 'She could scream, for all I care. I can't bear this playing dead.'

Crog held out the saucepan. 'Limpet?' he said.

'*No!*' snapped Wilf, louder than he meant.

He needed air. He opened the door, flung his arms wide and ran across the field and down to the beach. He stood at the water's edge, looking out across the grey sea and the pale dawn sky. There was nothing in the water. No boats. No helicopters. No one was coming. Not even *them*. Not yet.

He shut his eyes and took a deep breath. The air was very cold and smelled of the sea. It was as good a place as any for dying.

He thought, *It's going to be so hard without her.* How would he deal with Crog? And how could they live on in the wild? If he returned south, what on earth would he say to Dad? And Mr Robertson? What came into his mind were all those humdrum things that Ishbel did for him. Who would tell him now if his hair was wrong? Or his T-shirt naff? Who would monitor his washing? He always liked to have a faint smell of sweat on him; he thought it made him seem interesting and edgy. But who now was going to tell him when interesting and edgy tipped over into gag-inducing? And what was he going to do? He was an orphan. No mother. A father barely there. And now no twin. And Crog to look after. Crog. Was Crog going to be his new twin? That was an unbearable thought. Wilf scrunched up his eyes to stop himself crying.

Something scratched the rocks behind him. Wilf spun round, his nerves twanging.

But it was only Crog. Crog with a pail, squatting down by a rock pool.

'Crog! you gave me a fright! I thought you were *them*. Don't creep up on me like that!'

'The valley men will come. Always be ready,' said Crog.

'Thanks,' said Wilf coldly. 'I'll ask when I want advice.'

'We must be on our way soon. We have but one day and one night before the waters meet.' Crog had found a kitchen knife, and now he cut off a tendril of seaweed and dropped it into the pail.

'So, what's the seaweed for?' asked Wilf. 'I hate fancy food.'

'A strengthening drink for Ishie.'

'She's Ish*bel*. Ish*bel* to you. "Ishie" is just a family name,' said Wilf.

'Ishie,' said Crog quietly. 'Ishie, Ishie,' he repeated.

Wilf ignored this. 'Anyway, why are you bothering with seaweed? I thought you said she was going to die.'

'She will be needing her strength if she lives. She will be needing it yet more if she passes over.'

'I thought dying was the one thing in life that wasn't difficult. You croak, and then it's all over. No problemo,' said Wilf.

Crog gave a bitter little snort. 'That is but the beginning,' he said.

'So what's it like, then, being dead?' said Wilf conversationally. 'If that's not too personal a question.'

He thought, *I can ask anything now. We've nothing to lose.*

Crog lowered his eyes to the rock pool. Then he beckoned to Wilf.

'What is it?'

Crog beckoned again.

'What d'you want?' complained Wilf. 'I hate crouching down.'

Crog put his fingers to his lips and beckoned for a third time.

And finally Wilf gave in and went over. Together they leaned over the rock pool.

A small insect with a pod-like body was standing on the surface of the water.

'OK, a water boatman. A small brown bug. What's that got to do with anything?' asked Wilf.

'Look. Look another time,' insisted Crog. 'You will find that which needs seeing.'

Wilf looked more closely, and as he did so, the sun flickered over the rock pool. Was there one bug? Or two? He thought he saw a second bigger, darker bug suspended upside down in the water. Sometimes it was there. Sometimes not. He looked again. The smaller water boatman's legs were hair-thin, and where each leg rested there was a little concave dent in the surface of the water.

Wilf smiled. It was clever. The dents acted like lenses,

making the underwater reflection look bigger than the real insect. He leaned forward, casting his shadow over the water. The insect scuttled across the pool; so too did its underwater partner.

'It's a trick!' he exclaimed. 'The underwater bug is just a shadow.'

'The living are to us just as that fly on the water. Few know of the world of shadows at their feet.'

'You still haven't answered my question,' said Wilf. 'You haven't told me what it's like to be dead.'

'Dark and vast as the night sky,' said Crog.

'You've certainly got a way with words, Crog. But I mean, are there shops down there? Xboxes? Food?' said Wilf, feeling a little silly.

Crog grimaced. 'Different. As air is to water, or summer to winter, or day to night.' He laid a leaf very gently on the pond without breaking the surface tension, then continued, 'The water has a skin you cannot see that the flies walk on. So it is with this world and the next – there lies a skin betwixt the two. And that skin is as soft as duck down and as strong as bronze. That is whence the bowl gets its power. The bowl can break through that skin or send ripples across the surface. You are fortunate that you only held the bowl and did not drink from it – so you hear voices, and maybe you feel the presence of the dead and know of them around you. But those who drink from the bowl . . .' He stopped here and just shook his head sadly.

'*What?* What happens to them?' said Wilf. 'Crog? Crog?'

'If a man drinks from the bowl . . .' Crog paused theatrically. 'If he takes the water from the place of joining and sweetens it with mead and honey and drinks the bowlful, then he will be whole in both worlds.'

'Did you do that? Is that how you're here?' pressed Wilf.

Crog put his hand to his chest. 'I? Nay!' he said in a shocked voice.

'Yeah, but you're here, aren't you?'

'I rest here presently but I cannot stay. I am not whole. I rest here but for a short time – to bring the bowl to its place of ending.' Crog shook his head sadly, got to his feet and walked away.

A strange impulse took hold of Wilf. He knelt down and plunged his face into the clear, still rock pool. The water was so cold it seemed to burn his skin.

When Wilf and Crog returned to the house, Wilf was astonished to find Ishbel crawling very slowly and awkwardly towards the door. He thought, *If she's well enough to crawl, then she'll pull through.* As Crog held the door open, Wilf lifted her up and carried her outside. He held her while she groaned and her bowels emptied a runnel of green liquid onto the ground. Wilf was so pleased that she was better that he felt no embarrassment or disgust. He simply wiped her clean and then picked her up again. She fell asleep as he carried her back inside and then tucked her back into her bedding.

Ishbel slept through the rest of the morning, and Wilf woke her at lunch time. She groaned and didn't open her eyes. He tried to make her sit up, but her head drooped and he had to hold it up as he spooned in Crog's boiled seaweed potion. He didn't get far – her face puckered and she made retching noises. He laid her back down; almost immediately her breathing slowed again and she was asleep.

Crog, sitting with his knees up in a chair, watched all this. 'She's long a-dying,' he observed.

'Don't say that! She's getting better,' cried Wilf.

'Whichever the ways of the fate, we leave on the morrow.'

'She won't be better by then,' said Wilf. 'We can't just leave her here. What if *they* come and find her?'

'The earth gave her and the earth can take her back.

We make a bower in the woods, fill it with soft mosses and ferns.'

'*A bower!* A coffin, more like. You don't leave someone when they're like this.'

Crog shrugged. 'You stay, I go.'

'And take the bowl with you? You must be joking!' said Wilf. Why did Crog think he owned the bowl? It wasn't him who'd stolen it. Wilf looked over at him. He couldn't bear the sight of his horrible rope and his wizened little face and bony shoulders for a minute longer. He got up and strode up and down the study.

The rest of the afternoon passed slowly. Crog barely moved from his chair and kept his eyes fixed on the window, looking down towards the shore. Wilf fiddled interminably with the fire. He tried reading books from the shelves, but they were all old agricultural manuals or wordy memoirs, and when he opened them they breathed out mildew and boringness.

Meanwhile Ishbel got better almost as fast as she had fallen ill. At tea time she awoke and called for some sweet tea. Before Wilf could blink, she was sitting up and complaining about the state of the study.

Wilf offered her some soup.

'What's in it?' she said suspiciously.

'Cockles, limpets, little orange mushrooms, powdered oxtail soup.'

'Yuck.'

'I tell you, this is gourmet food,' he said. 'It would cost you a bomb in London to eat wild mushrooms and shellfish.'

Ishbel took a mouthful of soup, swallowed it and shuddered. 'Remember what Mum used to do when we were ill? She made us those ice lollies from fruit juice.'

'You don't get oranges or pineapples in these parts.' Wilf had no memory of the ice lollies.

'You know, it's been very strange,' said Ishbel. 'When I was really ill, I think I must have gone a bit mad.'

'Well, you did shout out,' said Wilf, looking over at Crog; he could feel him listening.

'I saw things,' she went on.

'What things?'

'I saw Mum. She came to me . . .' Ishbel struggled to find the words. 'She held me in her arms. There was a sort of softness, and then she vanished.'

Wilf felt sad. It seemed that Ishbel always got what he wanted most. She had all the memories. It just wasn't fair: all their shared past had been gobbled by Miss Photographic Memory, and he retained nothing.

And now *this*.

'What did she look like?' he asked. 'Did she say anything? What was she wearing?' A thousand other questions crowded into his mind.

'No. I can't remember . . . Something yellow, I think. But it was more a feeling. I just felt this love. It was as if I was at one with everything. And the room was shining. And suddenly I felt warm – as though there was a glow to everything. It was the best feeling ever. You can't imagine it.'

Ishbel smiled up at Wilf. 'At that moment, I just wanted to die.'

CHAPTER 19

W ilf lay in the dark with his eyes open. The night was passing agonizingly slowly. He had no idea how late it was – if only he still had his mobile – but at this rate, it would be centuries before dawn.

All his senses were alert. His mind was clear, his ears sharp. He could make out an occasional faint scrabbling in the corner. A field mouse? A rat? Hopefully a rat, for that would be bigger and have more meat on it. Then he thought, *I'm getting as bad as Crog. At this rate I'll be nibbling my own lice.*

Wilf tried changing position, wriggling round under his quilt for the umpteenth time, but he couldn't settle. *That's enough*, he thought. He cast his quilt aside and, stepping carefully over Ishbel and Crog, crouched down by the fire. He jiggled the embers with the poker, stacked a little wigwam of driftwood on top and blew on it. As the flames flared up, he burrowed away amongst the remains of supper and sucked on a forgotten mussel from the bottom of the saucepan.

What was he going to do? He was bored. His mind was empty. Ishbel had all those memories – those poignant little moments of childhood from the time before their lives had gone off course. And what did he have? Nothing. Yet he'd been there too. They were twins, after all. Twins are always together when they're little. Why did he not remember? What had happened to his memories of ice lollies, and butter churns, and felt mice? And this room? He had no memory of a book-lined study, yet he had probably eaten buttered toast by this very fireside. But he recalled nothing. He had nothing in his mind to shore him up, except that sad, melting feeling inside.

Tears of self-pity rolled down his cheek. He wiped his nose and looked over to check that the others weren't watching. Ishbel, weakened by her illness, was fast asleep. So was Crog. Usually he slept tightly curled in on himself – like the woodlouse he really was. But now his arms were spread out on either side, the box by his left hand.

The box . . . Wilf hadn't seen the bowl for some time now – the bowl that had caused them all this grief. After everything they'd been through, surely he deserved another look . . .

He crept up to Crog, then very gently picked up the box and brought it over to the fire. Crog barely stirred.

Wilf opened the lid. The box still smelled very faintly

of poor Gordon. There was another smell too – of something terribly old. He pulled back the straw and saw the rim of gold with its faint serrations. It was hard to imagine how something so fine and delicate could be made in a time before machines.

He held the bowl closer to the fire. The flames made the gold rim glimmer. He thought, *I'll just pour some water in and see how it looks – just a small amount*. He dipped the ladle into the pail by the fire and poured the liquid slowly into the bowl; he watched it settle in the bottom.

The bowl looked better with water in it. And surely a bowl ought to be used – not creepily hidden away in a hamster's travelling box.

Tentatively he took a sip. That was all right. And to hell with Crog. What had he been so worried about? It was hardly going to burn him. In fact, the water had slipped easily down his throat. So cool, so fresh, so clean.

This was just what he needed. He dipped the bowl directly into the pail and brought it out, heavy and dripping. A splash sizzled on the fire. Wilf glanced back over his shoulder, but Crog didn't stir. He raised the bowl to his lips and started to drink. He had forgotten about the crack, and the water leaked onto his hands and down his wrist. That meant he had to be quick. He went on drinking, the water flowing down his throat until the bowl was empty.

He shut his eyes for a moment and resisted the urge to retch. No wonder he felt a bit sick – that was far too much water all in one go. He slumped back against a chair leg, waiting for the queasiness to pass.

When Wilf opened his eyes again, something had changed. He felt decidedly odd; the air had a papery quality, as if the darkness in the room had been painted in and wasn't quite real. Just to be sure, he reached out to the grate, where the embers glowed a marker-pen orange.

What was happening? Maybe this was an after-effect of dehydration. He'd never really enjoyed drinking plain water, but there was nothing else – that was one thing about life in the wild: it was very short on energy drinks.

He needed, rather suddenly, to go to the bathroom. Still holding the bowl, he got to his feet, made his way to the side door and went out into the briny night air.

Wilf was relieving himself onto some tree roots when he first heard the singing. It was faint and far away, coming only in snatches. It sounded like church music. When he strained his ears, the singing seemed to fade away. Then a breeze would gust past him, bringing another snatch of song. Was it hymns they were singing?

Or was this all just his imagination? Or maybe more of those voices he'd heard in the cave . . . ?

The singing seemed to be coming from the sea. With the bowl tucked under his arm, Wilf walked quickly towards the shore, weaving his way round the hummocks in the field. As he stepped down onto the beach, the sound of the singing grew louder, as if welcoming him. The voices – he knew for certain now – were singing hymns.

Wilf stood at the water's edge, looking out at the still sea. On the strange rocky island, the castle was in darkness, but attached to one side – he hadn't noticed it earlier – was a small chapel with light now glowing in its windows. This was surely where the singing was coming from.

More than anything Wilf wanted to be near the singing. He wanted to be in that little chapel . . . though quite why this was so – normally he had no interest in church-going – he did not know. But he set off along the shore, and when he found their boat, he untied the mooring rope and laid the bowl down in the hull. Then, leaning his whole weight against the stern, he pushed and, slowly, crunching against the sand, the boat inched forward.

When it was afloat, Wilf climbed in, took up the oars and set off towards the island. He felt as if he were barely having to row, for the boat seemed to glide so easily – just like Crog's water boatman in the rock pool.

As the shoreline receded, he felt the dark sea and sky enveloping him. He kept rowing – the island was further out than he had thought, and the boat went slipping through a sea that rippled and moved and stretched out for ever.

Every so often Wilf turned to check his position and make sure he was still on course. After a long spurt of rowing he looked round, and suddenly the island seemed to have moved nearer. Next time he turned, it had taken another jump towards him. Now he could make out the contours of the castle, with its steep walls and thin slit windows and, below, the rock face that cut away down to the water.

He looked along the shoreline of sheer cliff, and there, at one end, was a small pebbly landing spot lit by the glow from the chapel windows. There were no other boats moored here; and only looking back later would he realize how strange that was.

Wilf rowed into the shallows and jumped ashore. As he landed, the singing stopped. He listened – and heard a man's voice, but it sounded far away and reedy. He couldn't make out the words.

The beach must have been a regular mooring place, for

he found a huge iron ring set into the rocks and looped the painter around it. Above him there was a steep slope up to the chapel, and he noticed the beginnings of a path that must once have zigzagged up between the rocks.

Holding the bowl tightly in his left hand, he set off. The way was overgrown, and climbing with just one hand wasn't easy. But he pushed his way forward, treading down thorns and clutching saplings to lever himself up.

At the top of the hill Wilf came out onto a windswept hummock of land and saw the chapel ahead of him. He rested behind a crooked tombstone and got his breath back after the climb. Long thin slices of light from the chapel windows illuminated the ruined graveyard around him. He could hear the congregation singing again now. And even though it was years since he'd last been in a church, he had some vague memory of the hymn – something about binding unto himself and the starlit heaven and the deep salt sea. He shuddered. If you were buried here, it would be a windswept eternity.

Wilf made his way round to the front of the chapel and found two huge studded wooden doors, thick with cobwebs. He turned the handle and slowly pushed one of them open.

The chapel was full – the congregation all standing, singing, with their backs to Wilf. At the front the minister, dressed in a long black cassock, was mounting the steps to the lectern.

Wilf glanced quickly to each side. No one had turned to look at him. He spotted a space in a pew near the back, and crept into it. He put the bowl down at his side and picked up a hymn book from the small shelf in front of him.

He glanced at the wispy-haired old man next to him to see which page to turn to. The man had a quavery thread of a voice and was holding his hymnal open with hands that were all bone and purple veins.

Wilf looked quickly away. He felt cold. Even though the chapel was full of people, the air remained clammy and unused. Maybe the congregation didn't come here often? Maybe, stuck out in the sea like this, the place could never warm up.

It was odd, though. And so was the singing. Why did it sound so thin?

Wilf stood up straighter and belted out the song with gusto. Volume had always been his strong suit, and even if he wasn't in tune, at least it would encourage the others to sing louder to drown him out.

He was still singing away stoutly when someone caught his attention.

A few rows ahead stood a teenage boy with a number

two crew cut and a most oddly shaped head – flattened at the back and sides as if it had been grown in a box. Some people never learn: it was just mental to keep your hair so short with a head like that – and with those crusty red bits of psoriasis too. Like wearing tight jeans if you had a fat bum.

Wilf narrowed his eyes. He'd know that head anywhere. Jonah O'Malley. But what was he doing here? Wilf looked again just to check. Yes, there it was: the tracking scar behind his left ear, and the little bald bump further up, where the edge of that bottle had clipped him. Poor old Jonah – always in the wrong place at the wrong time.

Wilf's mind halted. No! That wasn't right!

He clutched at the pew to keep himself upright. A feeling like the rising of a flock of birds surged up through his chest.

Jonah O'Malley was dead. He knew it. He'd even read it in the paper – his body had been hanging from the window bars of his cell in Juniper Down remand centre. Fourth inmate to die there that year.

Slowly, for he wasn't sure he wanted to look, Wilf swivelled his eyes around the chapel. Did he know anyone else here? He hoped not. But the beaky profile of an old woman in the aisle opposite did look familiar. And a few rows ahead he thought he saw the back of a black man in a dark blue jacket. That might be Jenkins.

Then he saw the splash of yellow. How could he have been in the chapel even a second without noticing it? There, standing near the aisle, was a slightly built woman with shoulder-length brown hair. She was wearing a bright yellow, sleeveless dress. He knew that yellow dress. Daffodil yellow, it was. And her arms were bare – Dad had always said Mum never felt the cold. She'd go barefoot on stone floors in winter.

The hymn ended, and the minister began a blessing while the congregation bowed their heads. All except Wilf. He didn't heed the minister's words, or the dust floating in the air, or the freezing draught. He just walked slowly up the aisle; nobody stopped him. His eyes were fixed on that yellow dress. As he drew near, he could see the freckles on the woman's arms.

About half a metre away, he stopped. He simply couldn't go any nearer. Would she look round? Would she sense that he was there?

In a tiny, creaky voice he said, 'Mum.' He waited, but nothing happened. She didn't turn round.

Wilf exhaled – he didn't know how long he'd been holding his breath; only that he felt dizzy. He blinked and willed himself to take a step forward. His feet simply wouldn't move.

He did the next best thing. Slowly and shakily, he reached forward. His hand hovered for a moment, and then touched that bare arm. Instantly he gave a start and moved his hand away. This wasn't a human arm – it was something waxy, a little stiff. Not warm. And very much *not* living.

He froze. What was he doing here? His mother had been dead and mouldering these last nine years. He wouldn't know her face if he saw it. How could he be such a fool!

That was the rule: never try for your true heart's desire. How had he *not* learned that? The only way was to hedge your bets. Keep your hopes low. Buy up Angel Islington, not Mayfair. Chat up the girl with the red nose and the hyena laugh, not the pretty one. Never, ever try for the real thing.

And this was the real thing, wasn't it? All he had ever really wanted. That loving and gentle embrace.

To Wilf's horror, the yellow dress rustled. She was starting to move. She was turning her head towards him! He caught a smell of raw meat. Dead meat. That wasn't how she should smell! In less than a second he would see her face, her eyes. It would be her – too close, too soon. Panic rose in him.

He turned and ran back down the aisle.

The congregation of the dead turned towards him, but no one stopped him. He flung back the great wooden doors, blundered across the little graveyard, and flew down that steep little path, ripping through the brambles. At the landing place he swore and hissed at himself as he fumbled with the mooring rope and pushed the boat down into the water. He rowed like a maniac, never flagging, never raising his eyes to look at the island.

He could have run a generator off the energy he was putting into the oars. Suddenly he felt tired. He slumped forward on the bench with his arms hanging loose and let the quiet of the cold sea embrace him. It was only now that he realized he had left the bowl back in the chapel. He thought, *I can't go back alone. Not with her there.* He rowed on into the dawn.

CHAPTER 20

As the boat approached the shore, Wilf saw what he first thought was an oversized cormorant hunched on a rock. It was Crog, all smouldering eyes and knobbly shoulders. The dawn light did him no favours.

Wilf thought, *Not now, Crog. I'm too tired.*

He brought the boat in closer, while Crog stared at him, then stepped out and dragged the hull up onto the beach, Crog watching his every move. He secured the rope, and still Crog's eyes never left him.

'Something got to you?' said Wilf, walking past him up the beach. 'Look any harder and your eyes'll wear out.'

'You drank from it,' spat Crog. 'Where is it?'

Wilf quickened his pace. Crog ran alongside him. 'Where *is* it?' he squealed. 'You made a vow!'

Wilf thought, *I can't face him now.* He hurried on towards the house, but Crog wouldn't be shaken off.

In the study Ishbel was sitting by the fire wrapped in a quilt. 'Where's the bowl?' she asked.

'Dunno.' Wilf crouched down by the fire. 'Glad you're feeling better.'

'Don't change the subject,' she said. 'Where's the bowl?'

'I said I don't know.' Wilf kept his eyes on the fire. He didn't have the heart or the energy to lie properly.

'You *don't know*?' Ishbel coughed for a moment and held her side. She sounded tired. 'There's no sign of you and the bowl has gone. Now you've come back, your hair is standing on end and you've got these mad staring eyes like you've just strangled a sack of kittens. What are we supposed to think?'

'You can think what you like. Anyway, aren't you meant to be ill?' Wilf prodded uselessly at the embers. 'Yesterday you were nearly dead.'

'Sorry to disappoint you,' said Ishbel. 'I'm feeling better now. Where's the bowl?'

'You vowed,' said Crog.

Wilf didn't answer.

'You broke a vow.' Crog's voice was almost a whisper.

'When? What vow?' said Wilf.

'That night. When we were journeying north. In the home that was not a home.'

'Oh *that*. Well, anything to get you off my back.'

'You made a vow,' persisted Crog. 'I failed afore, I cannot—'

'Stop it!' barked Wilf.

And Crog stopped. An uneasy silence followed. Tears slid down Crog's face, dropping softly off the tip of his nose. Wilf fiddled with the kindling. He wasn't going to look at Crog, but he saw the droplets splash silently onto the hearth. For someone so skinny and dried up, Crog produced amazingly large and lustrous tears.

Eventually Wilf could bear it no longer. 'OK,' he said angrily. 'Look, I'm sorry. I know it was wrong. If you want to hear what happened, I'll tell you.'

And he did. He recounted the events of the night as sketchily as he could. He couldn't bear to delve deeper. And how could he describe the fear he'd felt when he heard the rustle of his mother's dress?

Ishbel and Crog listened. When Wilf had finished, there was a long pause. Eventually Crog said, 'You drank only water from the bowl. With no mead and no honey. So you did not go beyond. All those you saw in the church were spirits called back by you, through the bowl. They were all spirits you'd once met in this life.'

'And that was quite scary enough,' muttered Wilf.

'You have learned your lesson,' said Crog a little priggishly. 'Now we must be returning.'

'Couldn't we just leave it there?'

Crog sniffed one of his long, thick sniffs. It meant 'No'.

'But it'll have gone by now.'

'Aye, true enough,' replied Crog with a baleful look at Wilf. 'Our chances are few. We'd sooner catch the west wind.'

'Oh, don't be so hangdog,' said Ishbel. 'Of course it'll be there. It'll be sitting on the pew where Wilf left it. Ghosts don't steal. Why would they? What good would it do them?'

And Wilf caught the glimmer of a sad, sly smile on Crog's face.

Ishbel sat in the stern with the quilt round her shoulders and Gordon's box by her side. Wilf and Crog rowed. Crog, wrapped up in his anger and his misery, wouldn't look at Wilf; wouldn't speak to him. And Wilf knew that Crog had staying power – his sulk would be monumental.

Wilf rowed a bit harder. At least that would take his mind off where they were going.

Eventually they came alongside the island, and the crags, covered in bird droppings, loomed above them.

'Wilf,' said Ishbel. 'There's one thing I don't get . . .'

'What's that?' he said warily.

'In the chapel, why did you do a runner? You

didn't even see Mum's face. Couldn't you have stayed?'

Wilf shrugged. 'Dunno.'

'*Dunno* isn't really good enough,' said Ishbel.

'Honestly, I don't. It was just too scary. She might have been anything. She'd have been all dried up, or something . . . something worse. And what if she *did* speak? All these years have passed. What could she say? What do the dead know about our lives now?'

Ishbel trailed her hand in the water. Wilf thought, *She doesn't want to go into that chapel any more than I do.*

'It must be horrible for them,' she mused, and gave a little laugh. 'What can they talk about? They're a bit out of the loop, aren't they? Like when you've been abroad and you go back to school, and everybody has been watching a telly programme you haven't seen.'

'Yeah,' said Wilf. 'But if I were dead, the one thing I'd let myself off would be school.'

'You do that anyway,' said Ishbel.

The tide was high so there was only a small patch of dry pebbles on the beach. Wilf heaved the boat out of the water and told Crog and Ishbel to go on ahead. Anything to give him more time. At least there was no singing now.

He sat down. Crog was out of sight, but Ishbel was still struggling up the rocks with the quilt around her shoulders. Eventually Wilf climbed up after them, trying to steady his nerves, plodding very slowly, panting like an old verger. The chapel door was open and he stopped on the threshold. Inside it looked so cool and peaceful, with the stained glass casting patterns on the stone floor.

Crog was sitting on a step by the altar, putting the bowl back into Gordon's box. Ishbel, still in her quilt, was sitting beside him. She smiled. 'It's all right,' she called out to Wilf. 'Nobody here. Only us. And the bowl.'

Her words echoed around the chapel, but Wilf remained rooted in the doorway. He knew it was good to have the bowl back, but his mind was far away. He could see that scene again: the old man with the veiny hands. And Jonah O'Malley. And Mum in that yellow dress.

He braced himself and walked in.

'There'll be a kettle somewhere, and biscuits if we're lucky,' said Ishbel.

Beside the chancel they found a locked room; Wilf took a small ivory bookmark from the lectern, slipped it into the door jamb and slid back the snib. Inside was a kitchen unit and a kettle. Wilf made tea, while Crog spooned the powdered creamer into his mouth. Ishbel started opening cupboards and found a row of black leather-bound books.

'What do you fancy? Births? Deaths? Marriages?' She ran her hand along the ledgers.

'Not marriages,' said Wilf. 'That's too soppy. Crog, leave some creamer for us.'

'How about deaths?' she went on. 'It's always interesting to know what gets you in the end.'

'You're a ghoul,' replied Wilf.

'We could see if Mum's in here . . .' She started to pull out the death registers. 'She died up in Scotland – that's why we're never allowed to come here now. And she could be here – it's so near the house.'

'*No!*' exclaimed Wilf. 'Sorry, I didn't mean to shout. Let's do births. Who knows, maybe this is where we were baptized. There can't be many churches around here.'

Ishbel pulled out the big, thick-papered birth registers. They smelled of glue, and the spines creaked when she opened them. The fourth volume was for the year of their birth.

She called Wilf over, and together, going back through the ledger, they ran their eyes down the pages. Suddenly Ishbel jabbed her finger by a double entry. There they were: *Ishbel Catherine MacGregor* and *Wilfred Edward MacGregor*. Both their parents had signed their names. Wilf inspected his mother's cramped, backward-sloping signature – perhaps she had been left-handed like him.

There was, he noticed, an asterisk by his name, and another by Ishbel's. And a footnote – a line of explanation at the end of the entry. It read *Frater trigeminus, mortuus natus, non baptisatus est.*

Why in Latin? Was it a prayer? Or something hidden?

He looked hard at each word, as if he could frighten the letters into fessing up their meaning. A couple of words he could guess. *Mortuus* must be 'dead'. *Baptisatus* was 'baptized'.

'What's *trigeminus*?' he wondered.

'*Gemini* is "twins", isn't it, like in the zodiac,' said Ishbel. 'And *tri* means "three" – like in "triangle" and "triathlon".' She paused. 'Must be "triplets".'

Then she gave a little guttural squeak. 'Look!' She pointed to each word in turn. 'Something . . . triplet . . . born . . . dead . . . not . . . baptized.'

'*Frater* is "brother",' said Wilf. 'So it's *Brother triplet born dead and not baptized.* Do you get it? We had a brother! A brother we never knew about!'

But Ishbel didn't answer. She was bent double with a fit of coughing. Wilf hoped she wouldn't be sick. Not here in the church – not over her own birth register.

Ishbel recovered, stood upright again and rearranged her quilt. Eventually she said, 'So we were meant to be three.'

'And having a brother would have changed everything,' said Wilf a little sadly.

'You'd still have been annoying.' She grinned at him. 'But I suppose from your point of view, I would have been outnumbered.'

'Why didn't we know about this?' said Wilf. 'How come no one ever mentioned it?'

'Well, who *would* have mentioned it? We're not exactly relative-rich, are we? And you can never get anything much out of Dad.'

'But what happened?'

'He's dead,' said Crog firmly. He'd put the jar of creamer down, but there was still powder around his mouth.

'Crog – what's wrong with you?' asked Ishbel. 'You look like you've swallowed a powder puff.'

He frowned. 'Powder puff?'

'A thing for dabbing make-up on with. Never mind!' said Ishbel. 'Let's go and see if we can find his grave.'

Outside, she wandered slowly from gravestone to gravestone, scraping away lichen and reading the inscriptions.

Crog sat on the grass, watchful and drawn in on himself, with the box close by his side. 'The moon this night will be but a thread. We must be starting the last furlong of our journey.' But Ishbel was out of earshot and Wilf, who was slumped on the ground nearby, ignored him.

Wilf didn't want to talk to anybody. He felt he needed a moment to take stock. He told himself he'd help Ishbel, but first he had to calm down. And the view did soothe him: the sea was all around – a great rippling cloth of grey beneath them. A dull sun loomed low in the south.

So he'd been here before, as a tiny baby. With Ishie. And maybe that other dead little body too.

Wilf felt a strange sorrow, like a stillness, settling over him. The entry in the register seemed to change everything. He was one of three, not two. He'd never put it into words, but he'd always thought his sense of loss – of needing more and always wanting more – stemmed from his mother's death. But maybe it went back further. How different things would have been if the family had been whole. If he had only had a brother. Someone who understood him completely. Someone to knock a ball around with. Or to bunk off school with. Or to do tricks and share the proceeds and have a laugh with.

But then Wilf wondered if his brother would have been rather different from him: perhaps a quiet computer geek. Maybe they could have gone into business together and done some lucrative hacking. Penetrated the Pentagon. Or snooped on NASA, or the FBI, or the

Wall Street investment banks. Serious money there.

Wilf was suddenly roused from his musings when Ishbel gave a cry and called him over. Where was she? He looked around and realized he'd lost track of time. While he had been daydreaming, she had worked her way across the graveyard and was now on her knees at the very edge, where the land fell away to the sea. Wilf scrambled to his feet and joined her.

She was bent over a small gravestone, set slightly wonkily into the ground. Something marked this grave out as different: standing with its arms resting on top of the stone, just like a regular customer at a bar, was an exquisitely carved angel.

Ishbel had scraped away the moss from the front of the gravestone. The inscription was terse: JAMES INNES MACGREGOR, and then his date of birth and death in Roman numerals. Underneath, near the feet of the angel, were carved the words: CALLED BACK.

CHAPTER 21

It was Wilf who suggested they should head north to the low blue hills in the distance. This was in quite the opposite direction to Crog's whirlpool – hopefully not what their pursuers would be expecting. Wilf's plan was that when they landed, they would hitch a ride south.

Crog said that whatever way they went, the men would be waiting at the crabwalk. He looked doubtfully at the sky, and even more doubtfully at Wilf. But eventually he relented, and they launched the little boat and headed off.

About a mile out to sea they came upon a sudden squall; the wind smashed icy rain into their faces and the boat lurched from side to side like a horrible fairground ride. Ishbel hid under her quilt – but soon it was soaked through and she threw it off. Meanwhile Wilf and Crog took turns on the oars, fighting against the weather and the sea. Wilf found that at least when he was rowing he could forget himself in the pulling back and forth. It was the staying still he couldn't bear – anything was better than just huddling up against the cold.

They rowed on and on, the coast never getting any nearer. For once it was Crog who took things hardest, saying repeatedly that their time was upon them, and that he had failed afore and could not fail again. At one point he completely lost his nerve, threw down the oars and burst into tears. Ishbel put her arm round his narrow shoulders and he leaned in to her, sobbing all the while. Wilf watched as a long skein of Crog's snot flew up and danced in the wind. He wished the Bronze Age had had handkerchiefs.

Eventually the wind died down and the rain petered out. A watery sunshine filled the sky and they began to make better progress. They reached the shore in the late afternoon, and pulled the boat up onto a shingle beach. Above them, facing out to sea, stood two white bungalows.

'We must be making haste,' said Crog. His eyes scanned the houses and the hill above them. He looked twitchy.

'Couldn't we pause for a breather?' asked Wilf. 'We could knock on one of those doors. I'm starving. They'll offer us drop scones. Or whisky – you'd like that, Crog.'

Ishbel rolled her eyes.

'Or those funny round Scottish cakes all covered in coconut,' added Wilf hungrily.

'What's got into you?' said Ishbel. 'D'you mean coconut snowballs? We're miles from any bakery. Anyone who lives in a little bungalow by the sea will not have coconut snowballs. They'll be reading the papers and watching the news. They'll recognize us immediately.'

'I could nick a car. That would get us there quicker.'

'Would that be before or after you've drunk their whisky and eaten their coconut snowballs?'

'You don't need to get snarky.'

'There are no people in the houses,' said Crog. He paused and then added, 'No people of quick blood.'

Ishbel grimaced but said nothing, and Wilf looked over at the dark windows of the bungalows. 'They must be holiday lets. There's not a light on anywhere.'

Crog headed off up the beach. And, yet again, Wilf and Ishbel found themselves running after him.

The front driveways of both bungalows were empty, and Ishbel insisted on stopping. 'I have to eat, and I must dry off or I'll get ill again.'

The idea of food cheered Crog and Wilf too. So they chose the most promising-looking bungalow, and Wilf manoeuvred up the kitchen window and let Ishbel and Crog into a faded little place that smelled of fried fish. The cupboards did not contain coconut cakes, but they found tea bags, a packet of cream crackers and some

UHT milk. Wilf lit the gas fire in the sitting room, and there they sat, drying off and dipping their crackers into mugs of tea. Ishbel curled up on the sofa and had a nap, but Crog couldn't relax. Wilf kept insisting that there would be plenty of time to get to the bridge, but eventually Crog sprang to his feet and jostled Ishbel awake.

'We go *now*!' he said.

As they climbed the hill behind the bungalows, they saw a thin moon in the afternoon sky, with Venus hanging a little way below. His voice cracking with emotion, Crog said, 'The night brings the high tide. When the waters meet. When my time comes upon me . . .'

They hurried on in silence, following the road as it wound along the side of the hill. Wilf felt very exposed. He searched the darkening sky, but there was nothing – no lights, and no sound except the occasional bleating of sheep. Why was he looking? He knew the men would attack without warning.

Suddenly Crog stopped. He crouched down, touching the tarmac with the palm of his hand. He paused a moment, gestured behind him and said, 'Car.' It was the first time he had used the word.

Wilf looked back down the road. There was nothing

but the grey-green outline of the hill. Eventually a pair of headlights appeared in the distance. They flashed, disappeared, and then came back a little closer. Now he could hear the engine. Wilf felt a flash of fear. Was it *them*?

The car came round the final bend. It was a big four-wheel-drive – not the sort of car he thought the men would use. And it was not going fast. No, this couldn't be *them*.

Wilf turned to Ishbel and gave her a little push. 'Get out in the road and wave like mad,' he said.

'Why me?' she asked.

'You're a girl. Everyone stops for girls! Just get out there!'

'Well, I'm leaving all the conversation-making and the lying to you.' She stepped out into the road and waved at the car. Wilf and Crog stood a little way back, waving too, like shadows behind her.

A couple of metres from Ishbel the car came to a stop, and a middle-aged woman with a neat bob of grey hair and a quilted jacket put her head out the window.

'We need a lift please,' said Wilf. 'We're doing our Duke of Edinburgh.'

She beckoned them in immediately.

The car was warm, dry, sweet-smelling. As Wilf slid into the front passenger seat, the woman flinched slightly.

'Where are you heading?' she asked.

'About twenty-five miles down the coast – the next small town. Where that big metal bridge is,' he replied.

She mentioned a name he'd never heard before.

'That's it,' he said firmly.

The car set off. The warmth was delicious, and his jeans started steaming.

The woman turned up the fan. 'Are you staying around here?' she asked.

'We're bivouacking out on the hills,' said Wilf. He liked the word *bivouacking*. It sounded authentic.

He wanted to look squarely at the woman – that was always more convincing. But what if she recognized him from the newspapers? Better to stay in profile. He kept his eyes on the road ahead.

'We're on our very last module of the Duke of Edinburgh,' said Wilf.

'Ah,' said the woman. 'Which one? Bronze? Silver?'

'Gold.'

'Aren't you a bit young?' she wondered.

'Oh, we're older than we look,' said Wilf quickly. Then he added, 'We're doing environment and survival. They drop you off in the middle of nowhere and you have to fend for yourself. You know – live off berries and song thrushes.'

'Goodness!'

'We ate squirrel last night. Not much meat on them. But quite tasty, you know.' He was beginning to enjoy himself, but heard a little intake of breath from Ishbel.

Maybe the woman heard it too – for she glanced over her shoulder. Ishbel smiled back at her angelically. Crog merely stared vacantly ahead. The woman looked at him again.

Crog smiled, giving a full display of blackened stumps.

The woman clutched the steering wheel tightly and drove on.

CHAPTER 22

The hills levelled out and they came down towards the estuary. Wilf realized that, despite Crog's complaints, the bridge was in fact beautiful: a graceful fretwork of metal that spanned the water at the narrowest point, where the estuary met the head of the loch.

The woman dropped them off on the far side of the bridge. The road led up through a village and they hurried into an alleyway between the houses. Here Crog instantly pressed himself up against the wall.

'No one saw us,' he panted. It was really a question.

'The street's nearly dead.' Wilf sneaked a view round the corner of the building. 'Just a chip shop and some old geezer walking his dog.' But the dog, a beagle, had taken fright. It was barking and jumping off the ground on all fours as if an electric current ran through the pavement. The old man was looking up and down the street to see what had frightened it.

'We must make haste,' said Crog above the barking. 'The tide is coming to the ebb.'

They ran down the alley and, at the end, turned into a lane that sloped down behind the backs of the houses. Keeping close to the wall, they crept along. Wilf thought, *If there are any dogs here, they will go mental when they smell Crog.* And just then, it happened: a dog behind the wall howled.

They ran on, the howling gradually dying away behind them. At the end of the lane, they came to the shore and took cover behind some concrete bins. Above them, the girders of the bridge were floodlit, a shining cat's cradle casting a weird illumination over the shore and the black water below.

Wilf heard a scrabbling sound. He thought, *Rats*, but it was just Crog ripping open the Velcro tabs of his photographer's waistcoat. After a bit of wriggling he brought out some sachets of white sugar and a can of alcohol-free lager.

'Hey! Where've you been hiding that? I could do with a drink. Or at least some sugar,' said Ishbel. She was squinting – Wilf knew her eyes always went a bit out of kilter when she was tired.

Crog didn't seem to hear what she'd said. Carefully he took the bowl out of the box, and put the can of lager and the sachets inside it. His breathing was juddering, his little pigeon chest moving up and down as his eyes panned along the waterfront. Then, in a slow, solemn voice, he said, 'Ishie, Wilf . . . our journey together now is ended. This I do alone.'

He nodded once to Ishbel and once, more curtly, to Wilf. His farewell completed, he stepped out from behind the dustbins and walked down towards the shore.

Wilf and Ishbel watched him go.

'We should really stop him,' said Ishbel. 'He said the men would be here. He'll get his eyes gouged out.'

'We can't. It's none of our business.' But Wilf knew she was right. The men would be there, somewhere.

'Did you see him welling up? Poor little thing,' murmured Ishbel.

'Poor little us too if they get hold of us. And what's he got that sugar and lager for?' Wilf knew then that he was being slow and stupid. Something was happening that he didn't understand, something that was almost certainly not good. If only his wits were sharper. 'And where is this whirlpool? Don't you think it's a bit weird?'

'Everything is a bit weird,' said Ishbel. 'But there is a perfectly rational explanation for the whirlpool. Listen: if the tide is very low, the level of the sea could become lower than the level of the loch. Then the fresh water from the loch would empty into the sea. As salt water has a higher density than fresh water – Wilf, you'll remember that from chemistry if you were listening, or were ever there in the first place – the salt water will push the fresh water up out of the way. Ergo a whirlpool.'

'Don't *ergo* me,' said Wilf.

'*Ergo* is Latin for "therefore".'

'Shuddup.'

But Ishbel wasn't listening. She gave a gasp, and Wilf turned and saw what she had seen: a ridge of high water travelling along the still surface of the loch, like a snag in a stocking. Only this was fast, and noisy too. As the wave approached, it picked up speed and gave a muffled roar.

It was getting bigger too. And just as it drew level with Wilf and Ishbel's bins, the moment came when the wave suddenly folded in on itself, forming a churning, spitting mass of foam and black water.

'There are his wild dogs for you,' said Ishbel in a hushed voice. 'I see what he means.'

'He's right, though, isn't he?' whispered Wilf. 'That would pull a man down easy-peasy. If he goes anywhere near it, we'll never see him again.'

And Crog? Wilf scanned the shore, and there he was squatting on the pebbles with the bowl and the can of lager in front of him. He was ripping something open with his teeth.

'It'll be those sachets of sugar he nicked,' said Ishbel.

Crog emptied the sachets into the bowl. Then he lifted the ring-pull on the can of lager and poured in the liquid.

'At least we've taught him something,' said Wilf. 'He didn't know what a can was. Remember how I had to show him?'

'Yes!' said Ishbel sourly. 'And look where it's taken us. We'll never see him again . . .'

Sugar and lager. Suddenly Wilf understood. He gave a groan of rage.

'What is it?' asked Ishbel.

'Sugar and lager – that's the nearest he could get to honey and mead. All that stuff he told us about casting the bowl into the waters was just nonsense. He's doing what he told me no one should ever do. He's going *to drink from the bowl*!'

Wilf stared hard at the spindly little figure by the shore. Crog had fooled them. He'd got them to do his bidding, wound them round his little black fingers. And Wilf had been such an idiot! He'd handed that bowl over, meek as a lamb.

'He told me never to drink from the bowl,' hissed Wilf. 'He said holding the bowl was bad enough, and drinking water from it like I did meant I'd be at one with the dead. To drink honey and mead from the bowl at this place and time was to become whole in both worlds. He made it sound terrible, and now that's just what he's going to do!'

Wilf lunged forward, but Ishbel pulled him back behind the bins. 'Don't!' she whispered.

'I'm going to smash his face in!' Wilf tried to struggle free, but she held him tight. 'I'm going to wring his scrawny little neck.'

'You won't have to. *They*'ll do it for you.'

'*What?*'

'See for yourself,' said Ishbel. '*They*'re coming.'

Crog was wading out into the falls, the bowl held high above his head. He was already up to his thighs, and his body was swaying as the water pushed against him. Only a couple of metres more and he'd be in the whirlpool.

And beyond Crog was something else: a small moving group of lights down amongst the stanchions under the bridge. Then Wilf heard, above the churning of the water, the sound of an engine. And suddenly the lights were coming nearer and he realized that they were part of a motorboat. In the boat were three figures, and as the boat shot forward, they came into view: a small, elderly woman wrapped in a shawl and two men in wetsuits. The men were well-built, muscular.

It was Snout and Badger.

Crog heard the motor too, and with the bowl between

his hands, he stretched his arms out in front and plunged forward. But the men were quicker. The boat skidded to a stop, and Snout slipped over the side and grabbed Crog by the back of the neck just as he brought the bowl down towards his lips. With his other hand Snout took the bowl and very carefully handed it up to Badger. And all the while Snout held Crog up as he kicked and thrashed and tried to wrestle free.

Then Badger turned off the engine, and the old woman, her long white hair now uncovered, stood up in the middle of the boat. Badger handed her the bowl. At this point Crog made what Wilf immediately understood to be a terrible misjudgement and gave a high-pitched squeal of anger. It stopped suddenly – for Snout thrust his head under the water and held it there.

At first Crog's arms and legs splashed and thrashed, but gradually the movement stopped. Snout never so much as moved his arm or seemed to notice him. Nor did the old woman pay him any attention. As he drowned, she slowly and carefully inspected the bowl. She turned it round in her hands, stroking the wood, and holding it against her cheek.

Behind the bins, Wilf put his knuckles in his mouth and bit down hard. He was aware of Ishbel, very still beside him, her breath sobbing. Tears ran down Wilf's face. His anger at Crog for tricking them and taking the bowl from him was gone. If he'd been Crog and had come across a pair of green teenagers, all softened up by modern life, wouldn't he have done the same?

And now Crog was getting his just deserts. Poor Crog. Wilf knew that he and Ishbel should run away now. But it was too late to run. Too late for Crog too. Wilf thought, *God have mercy on lying, thieving Crog*. And loathing himself for his cowardice, he huddled next to Ishbel. He clenched his eyes, and his face and his whole body. He waited.

CHAPTER 23

'He's still holding him under,' Ishbel whispered. 'Oh God!'

Crog's life – or his afterlife, or however you defined it – was coming to an end. This was surely murder, a careless, casual extinction. Reluctantly Wilf opened his eyes. He *had* to do *something*. Scream? Shout? Run down and get his eyes gouged out too? No, he couldn't.

After an eternity, the old woman seemed to finish her inspection. She dipped a finger into the liquid, sucked it and nodded approvingly to Badger. Slowly she stood up and held the bowl high above her head. Wilf saw her lips move – she was saying some sort of prayer or incantation. When she finished, she lowered the bowl, took a mouthful of liquid, and then poured the remainder into the churning water. Afterwards she sat down again, holding the bowl in her lap.

The ritual seemed to be over. Badger started the engine, and Snout casually raised his arm, lifting a sodden bundle out of the water. Crog's head hung down onto his chest. His limbs were entirely still. Snout, still using just one arm, cast the body towards the beach as if he were throwing away an old apple core. Then he climbed back into the boat, and they sped off towards the open sea.

Wilf and Ishbel didn't wait. They ran down to the waterfront and waded into the water. From the stern, Snout was watching them, but as the boat swooped under the bridge, he turned his head away.

Crog was spread-eagled face down in the water, limbs floppy. Wilf and Ishbel dragged him up onto the shore and held him upside down. They squeezed his stomach, whacked him in the small of the back, pumped his chest, turned him over time and time again like a fish on a griddle.

At last Crog gasped, and Ishbel and Wilf moved him onto his side. Barely raising his head, he was sick onto the pebbles. Then he just lay there with his eyes shut, his shoulders heaving, tears and snot running down his face.

Wilf stood back, his arms crossed. 'I'm waiting,' he murmured.

'Waiting for what?' said Ishbel.

'Waiting for him to be a bit better. Then I can throttle him.'

After a while Crog sat up, still snivelling. He pushed the matted hair off his face. His features were now red and puffy – drowning had at least put a bit of colour in him.

He looked at Ishbel and smiled meekly. Then he caught Wilf's eye and his mouth crumpled. He knew what was coming. Wilf grabbed him by his kaftan, hauled him up and shook him till his eyes rolled.

'Stop!' cried Ishbel. 'You'll break his spine.'

Wilf threw Crog down onto the pebbles and kicked him hard. 'He hasn't got a spine to break,' he said in disgust.

Crog lay curled up, head tucked in.

Wilf leaned over and shouted in his ear. 'You were trying to drink from that bowl. That's what you told us never to do! What's your game?'

There was no answer.

'Say something!' yelled Wilf, and gave him another kick.

Crog's voice was tiny and snot-filled. 'What did they do with the bowl?' he asked. 'Did they throw it into the falls?'

'No,' said Wilf. 'They're not that stupid. They took it with them.'

Crog let out a thin wail. 'Gone!' he cried. 'Gone!'

Wilf kicked him again. 'Yes, they took it – and why didn't they *murder* you while they were at it? Why didn't they pull your eyes out, like they did Jenkins?'

'You can hardly blame him for not being dead!' said Ishbel. She added uncertainly, 'Or half dead – or whatever he is.'

'Oh yes I can!' said Wilf. 'If he'd stayed in his bog, none of this would have happened! Jenkins wouldn't be dead. I wouldn't have to lose my suspended – I'll go into remand home for this. And prison later, when they pin Jenkins on me. We wouldn't have been chased across Britain. We wouldn't have walked out on everyone and everything in our lives. Have you thought of that, eh?'

'But it was *you*, Wilf!' shouted Ishbel. '*You* stole the bowl.'

'Yeah, but that's not the point!' he said angrily.

'It *is*,' she insisted. 'And you're not the only thief around here. Did you notice something? Those men and that old woman, they acted like *they* owned the bowl. They weren't stealing it. They were taking it back. It was *theirs*.'

Wilf looked down wearily at the wet huddle of limbs at his feet. Of course, it all made sense. He said quietly, '*You* are the thief, not *them*. You stole that bowl from *them*.'

Crog was dogged. 'I took it.'

'It was *theirs*.'

'Only when they held it. When I held it, it was *mine*.'

'You're a thief!' said Wilf, outraged.

'And thee?' muttered Crog.

'He's got a point, Wilf,' said Ishbel. 'Takes one to know one.'

'Yeah, but there's meant to be honour among thieves!' said Wilf. 'You deceived us. Ishie and I, we looked after you. We fed you. We clothed you. We got you out of London, came all the way up here. And this is how you treat us?'

Crog began to cry.

'And don't snivel! Couldn't resist it, could you? You were going to drink from it, weren't you? That's what all that hokum with the sugar and the lager was all about. You were wanting to come back and be one of us for ever. Have a flushing toilet and eat chips and fudge. That was it, wasn't it?'

'Let me be!' wailed Crog.

'Why *did* you want to come back?' asked Ishbel, far more gently.

'Why should my bones lie cold?' Crog wiped his nose on the sleeve of the kaftan. 'I never drank the sweetness of life! I was aye small and underfed and poorly fashioned. With the bowl I could return for true. Hale and sound and whole of limb. I'd be able to eat meat, bear arms . . . one day love a maid, maybe father wains.' He rested his head on his knees and gave a long trawling sniff. 'Now there is nothing. Now death gnaws at my marrow and I drink but the dregs. My time will soon be upon me.'

Wilf sucked his teeth. The rage had drained out of him again. Now he just felt tired.

'We all need a bit of food to perk us up,' said Ishbel soothingly. 'I'm starving. Why don't we go back to the village? There was a chip shop, wasn't there? Let's get some chips.'

'Yeah,' said Wilf. 'A fish supper.'

Crog brightened at the idea. 'Yes. A fish supper. A last supper.'

They walked back up to the village. There was no sign of the police or even any people, apart from two slightly drunk women walking arm in arm down the road. Ishbel used her last soggy twenty-pound note and they bought three haddock and chips, with a pickled egg on the side for Crog.

Crog said he wanted to go to the woods, and so, carrying their packets of fish and chips, they continued on up the high street past the last houses. When the road turned down towards the coast, they took a path into a forestry plantation. A little way up they came to a bench overlooking the estuary, and here they sat down to eat their suppers.

Darkness was creeping in from the sea and now a scattering of lights had come on down in the village. Wilf could still just about make out Crog and Ishbel sitting at his side. He felt cheered by the warm chips on his lap.

For some time they ate in silence.

'I think it's time you came clean, Crog,' said Ishbel. She'd finished and was scrunching her chip paper into a ball.

'Come clean?' Crog sounded puzzled.

'Yeah. Tell us what really happened,' said Wilf. 'Tell us the truth about stealing the bowl.'

Crog bowed his head. His hand scrabbled in the bottom of the chip paper, searching out crumbs which he ate slowly and carefully. Finally he began:

'The bowl is not from my days. It came from the far-off times of the great oaks, just as I told you. They say that in those times the land and the skies and the winds were at our behest. The birds in the air, they sang for us, and the rivers gave us their little silver fish.'

'What are you driving at?' said Ishbel.

'The bowl . . .' Crog sucked the salt off his fingers. 'I'm talking of the bowl. And the bowl, like all things, holds to its origins. It ties us to the past and to the dead, but it gives also a little of the goodness of those times. Those who have the bowl do not starve. Their cups are full—'

'I was pretty hungry up in the hills,' Wilf pointed out.

'We had the tree rats,' countered Crog.

Wilf remembered the scrawny little squirrel corpses. There would have been more meat, he thought, on Gordon. He rubbed his eyes. He wished he hadn't thought of Gordon.

'The men that track us with fire and blood,' continued Crog, 'they are valley people. And the valley people . . . in my days they held the bowl and its good things came to them. They were fair of face and sturdy-limbed. They lived long and well off the fat of the land. They ate meat and curds. My people, for we were without the bowl, grew small and lean – there was nothing but gristle and shellfish for us. We were always hungry. In the grey furrow of spring, when the shores were picked clean and the game was thin, we lost our wains and our venerables. We were cast adrift.

'Some, goaded by their hunger, joined these valley people. But then they were lost to us – they worked as slaves, beaten for idleness. They slept far from the hearth. For the valley people took us for vermin. They wouldn't even lie with our women.'

Wilf needed something to do. He picked up a stick and threw it down the hill towards the village. It landed somewhere below with a faint thump.

Crog resumed his tale. 'Most of us remained wanderers, up in the mountains or down by the shore. We too wanted the good lands, the meat and the curd. But we had neither the strength nor the numbers for war.

'When I came to be born, as I told you, it was on the tide line. I was small and stealthy and supple. My mother tutored me well. I learned grace from the swallow, watchfulness from the falcon, speed from the hare, patience from the dead man's hound.

'If I and my people were to be strong, I knew we must take the bowl. I knew how to do so too – for we had watched the valley people many times. Twice a year, at the neap tides, they made the journey down to the shore and set up camp there. One of their venerables, an old wise woman, would bring the bowl inside a casket. When the waters stirred – as they have stirred tonight – the valley people would start to sing the songs and the wise woman would take the bowl from the casket. She would pour honey and mead – the good gifts of this world – into the bowl. Then, as the people stood along the shoreline, she would walk into the water carrying the bowl high above her head. The singing would become louder and higher until she reached the falls. There, where the water was turning, she would dip the cup into the water, and while the people cried out to the skies, she would drink from the cup. Just one mouthful. The rest she poured away. Afterwards, when the wise woman came ashore, they feasted by the waterside and slept long into the morning.

'There came the year when I was ready.' Crog tucked his hands under his thighs and went on with his story, rocking slightly back and forth. 'I chose the spring tide. I knew I must keep my bowels empty and my spirit clean, so for two days I did not eat, nor did I drink. When the eve of the spring tide came, I climbed a pine tree down by the waterside and waited. Everything went as it always did. The valley people came, and the waters stirred, and the wise woman waded out with the bowl of honey and mead and drank her mouthful and returned. Afterwards the feasting began: the people roasted venison and drank their mead and made merry. All that time I was up in the pine tree, still as an adder. Oh, how it was . . .'

Here Crog shook his head and smiled sadly. 'The smell of the meat was so sweet and how my belly ached. But I kept my peace and waited.'

'Then what happened?' asked Wilf eagerly. He had got to his feet and was now pacing back and forth.

'Late in the night,' said Crog, 'just before the dawn, the last reveller fell into the arms of sleep. Then I climbed down from the tree. I walked sly and silent towards where the wise woman slept with the bowl in her arms. I moved a willow branch aside and the night breeze crossed her face and she stirred in her sleep. I took the bowl from her arms. Then I ran.' He paused, his back now hunched over a little more.

'And then?' prompted Ishbel.

'Then I fell,' said Crog. 'My foot caught on a tree root. It may be that my blood was too thin from the fasting. Or the dark night and the silence had stirred my wits . . .' He gave a shrug. 'I know not. I know only that I fell and, as I fell, the bowl rolled out of my hand and hit a rock and a piece of the wood broke away. The cracking of the bowl awakened one of the sleepers, who roused the wise woman. She let out a scream that would split the world asunder. Then everyone was awake. I hid in a gorse bush, but they soon found me. They beat me. They bound me and then . . .' Crog looked down at the rope round his neck and fiddled with the frayed ends. 'They brought me low.'

'What d'you mean?' asked Wilf.

Crog looked at him glumly. 'They slayed me.'

'How? With that rope?'

'Wilf! Stop interrupting!' said Ishbel.

'They slayed me thrice,' said Crog matter-of-factly. 'They poisoned my guts with henbane. They stove my skull in with a rock. They ended by hanging me high from a tree.'

The silence that followed was like a stone dropping down a bottomless well.

Ishbel shifted uncomfortably. Eventually Wilf said, 'Three deaths – it's pointless really. A bit like getting concurrent prison sentences. Why did they do it?'

Crog fiddled again with his frayed ends. 'One death for the theft of the bowl. One death for the crack in the bowl. One death for the missing piece. The missing piece was the worst. The people were angry. The bowl was broken and it couldn't be made whole, on account of the missing part. Just one piece of wood was missing. And now the bowl's powers would always be weakened, and the crops would be less and the cattle thinner – even if they found the missing part. The people looked everywhere. They cut down the bushes and shook them. The women took the combs from their hair and passed them through the grass. They were on their knees, looking and looking. They searched everywhere and they could not find the missing piece. But . . .' Crog paused. 'There was one place they did not look.'

Crog opened his mouth, and with his forefinger he delved along the bottom line of his gums and hooked out a dark, wet triangle about two centimetres long. He held the fragment up. It was exactly the shape of the crack Wilf had seen in the bowl, only so blackened and slimy that it hardly looked like wood at all.

'Is this it?' said Wilf. 'You've kept it there all this time!'

Crog smiled mysteriously. 'No. Not for sleeping – I might choke. And when the valley people searched, I swallowed it. It passed through me while I was their prisoner.'

'Yeuch!' said Ishbel.

'Yes,' replied Crog, misunderstanding Ishbel's disgust. 'It was sharp. I bled. But it meant that the bowl was still mine. It let me know . . . it drew me to where the bowl was. With this piece, I could find the bowl again.'

'I see. So that's how you found me. It's like your own personal radar?' said Wilf.

'Radar?'

'Forget it.'

'What were you saying, Crog?' said Ishbel.

'All the time the valley people searched. And all the time, the wise woman – she knew I had the piece. She looked at me. She knew, but she was silent.'

'Why didn't she say anything?' asked Ishbel.

'She was a wise woman,' replied Crog. 'She understood that the wood would lodge in my heart as a canker and speak to me always of what I had lost. So I would never rest. I would not sleep the sleep of the dead. I would always be wanting. I would not live or die. I would belong to neither world. I would try to return here, but I was aye poorly fashioned, a thin scrap of a thing that could never thrive. When the bowl was brought out of the water – that was half a year ago – it became easier. I had more strength to me when I returned this time.'

'Was that the same old woman we saw in the boat?' asked Ishbel. 'The one who took the bowl?'

'It was. I hoped she would cast the bowl back into the water. But she will take it somewhere lost to men, dead or alive. The story is over. No one now will find it and hold it and drink from it and flourish from its power.'

Crog snapped his fingers together wetly. 'The killings, all three killings, took a trice. Even the poisoning spanned but one long night. But wanting is an eternity. The very worst of punishments.'

Wilf stood up and paced around the bench. He looked down the hillside to where the lights of the village glittered like stars. Beyond, the sea spilled away into blackness.

'So when did you come here?' he asked. 'To this world, I mean?'

'At first light. At the dawn of day,' said Crog. 'I came directly to your high house.'

'You didn't meet the men beforehand? You didn't have a fight with them?'

'Nay,' replied Crog, puzzled by the question.

'So you just arrived in my bedroom?' said Wilf. A most unpleasant suspicion was forming in his mind.

'Where? Your chamber?' said Crog. 'I was at the lintel of your high house. Then I climbed the steps and came to you.'

Wilf remembered that morning. He'd woken, and there was Crog in the corner of his bedroom with the trickle of red and brown liquid winding slowly across the floor. There had been blood on Crog's fingers. Not old, brown blood. Bright red, fresh blood.

Wilf turned and looked at him. 'It was you! You did it! *You* murdered Jenkins. I saw your hands.'

'The guard at the door?' said Crog coolly. And it seemed to Wilf that he spoke as if he had killed many people and was just wanting to clarify precisely which victim they were talking about.

'Yes,' said Wilf flatly. 'Jenkins was the doorman. We've known him for years. His wife used to make us our tea.'

'He did not give me entry,' Crog explained.

'That doesn't mean you had to kill him!'

Crog looked away evasively. 'He had by his chair a small green thing, and when I pressed it the doorway opened itself. When I climbed to your house, I pressed no green thing, for the door was open.'

'My fault,' murmured Ishbel. 'I hate carrying keys when I go for a run.'

But Wilf hardly heeded her. 'Crog, what I want to know is why couldn't you have killed him *properly*? Shot him or something. Not gouged his eyes out.'

'Only *they* have guns. *They* have cars. As old owners, their ties to the bowl were stronger than mine and its call to them was stronger. Thus they came afore – when the bowl was first lifted from the water half a year hence. When those people searched the falls with a rod that heard the gold and they brought it up.'

'That'll be the archaeologists,' said Ishbel quietly.

'So the valley men had from the waning of the year until now to learn your ways. The old woman likewise. They had time and they had gold. They are rich, *always* rich,' said Crog with sullen emphasis. 'My ties were weaker, so I was more lately come – just on the morrow when you met me. And I have no guns, no machines. I am poor.'

Crog addressed Ishbel now. 'And I am weak. The weak must always attack the soft parts. The eyes, the groin pouch . . .'

Ishbel grimaced. 'Crog, you're hardly *weak*!' she said.

But Wilf couldn't even look at Crog. That faint smirk of his really was detestable.

CHAPTER 24

Wilf sat mute and mortified on the bench. He saw with a horrible new clarity his own foolishness and failures of judgement. In the museum, why hadn't he just let the bowl be? He should have known that shut-down security sensors were *not* a personal invitation to him. All along, he should have smelled a rat. A thin, bony 3,000-year-old rat with a sneaky, rat-like cunning.

Wilf knew Jenkins's death was partly his fault. What was the technical term? *Accessory to a murder*, or something along those lines. You could get eight years, or ten, or even twelve for that. And trying to wriggle out by saying that the real perpetrator had come from the Bronze Age – well, then you'd serve your time in a psychiatric unit.

He tried to shake off these thoughts. He told himself not to dwell on the future. He looked out into the darkening night, hoping for distraction. But there was nothing. Down in the village it was bedtime and the lights were going out one by one – like so many eyes closing.

A bat the size of a hand veered past Wilf's face.

Horrified, he lurched backwards. As he fell, he reached out for the bench – the empty bit where Crog had been sitting.

'Where's Crog?' Wilf reached out again. His hand met air. 'Ahh! He's slunk off with that creep-up-on-you walk of his.'

'Probably having a pee,' said Ishbel tiredly.

They waited. Small animals scurried nearby, but Crog didn't return.

'Maybe he's just nodded off in some corner,' said Ishbel. 'Crog can sleep anywhere. He can probably sleep standing on one leg, like a stork.'

'He has disappeared before. Remember when we were at the show house?' said Wilf. He added quickly, 'Not that I care – after everything he's done.'

'One thing about our Crog,' said Ishbel. 'He's always a lovely bag of sunshine and surprises, isn't he? It's like a black widow spider waiting under your toilet seat. Our own little anchovy-flavoured jelly bean.'

'I thought it was only me who hated him,' said Wilf.

'Huh!'

'So . . . are we going to look for him? He isn't worth it, but we can't just let him drift off.'

'I know,' Ishbel said. 'It's ridiculous, but I still feel a bit responsible for him. And at least the search will warm us up.'

She went back towards the road, and Wilf entered the woods behind them. In the trees it was too dark to see much, so he fumbled and stumbled, his arms and legs catching on branches. Twigs cracked. How had Crog spirited himself away so soundlessly?

Yet there was a way through – part of the undergrowth was easier to push back, allowing Wilf to plough forward. At last he saw a faint glimmer of light coming from deep among the trees up ahead. He held his breath and listened. Nothing.

Was it Crog? Who else could it be? Drawn by the light, Wilf went on, zigzagging from one shadowy tree to the next. Up ahead, he saw a clearing. He craned his neck and looked in.

Crog lay at the foot of a massive tree, seemingly asleep, and the light came from a torch lying by his hand. When had Crog got himself a torch? *Another thing he's nicked behind my back.*

Slowly Wilf approached. Crog looked awfully still and small. Not himself somehow. Not right at all.

Wilf picked up the torch and shone it in Crog's face. Crog didn't flinch. His eyes were closed, his lips and the tip of his nose bluish, as if he were shutting down from the outside in.

Or was he already dead?

Carefully Wilf touched Crog's cold cheek.

A grubby hand reached out towards him.

'I failed,' said Crog, with just a scratch of voice. He didn't open his eyes.

'Not entirely,' said Wilf. 'You certainly had us fooled.'

Crog smiled faintly. 'Aye, you drank that tale as warm broth.'

'We certainly did.' Wilf could smell the pickled egg on Crog's breath. 'But I don't suppose "sorry" is in your vocabulary, is it?'

Crog ignored this. 'I cannot stay. I go now.'

'Crog, we've come all the way here with you,' said Wilf. 'Don't leave us now.'

'Cover you me over with leaves . . . Leave me not for the buzzards.'

'You can't just die!' cried Wilf.

'Not die. Go . . .' Crog murmured something else that he didn't catch.

'What was that?'

But there was no response. Crog's shoulders sank back against the tree trunk and his mouth fell open, revealing a solitary brown molar.

Crog was finished. Used up. Dead.

CHAPTER 25

Wilf felt empty and underwhelmed. Above all, he felt wronged. This was another loss. Crog had gone, and the bowl had gone, and the brother he'd never known had gone. And his mother had gone, and with her had gone too the sense of being part of a *proper* family.

Also a tiny, not good part of Wilf had hoped for more with Crog's death. Some drama maybe? But there'd been nothing. Just a sag of the shoulders, and Crog had gone and left them. How typical was that? Crog was such a rip-off. Even his death was a disappointment.

Was he truly dead? Wilf propped up one of Crog's eyelids with his forefinger, and shone the torch in on a black pupil. A tiny version of his own pug-ugly face looked back at him, as in a fairground hall of mirrors. Now he knew what the dead saw: glaring white light and freakshow noses.

He let Crog's head fall back, and then he wept. He wept out of pity for Crog, and for himself, and for Jenkins, and for Ishbel, and for this cold dark night and all the cold dark nights to come. And when eventually he was all cried out, he lay back in the leaves and shut his eyes and wished for a cigarette.

He thought, *Now we can go home*. But home to what? Home to school? Home to Dad, even though he was never there? Home to Mr Robertson and the Youth Offending Service? Perhaps Mr Robertson would be understanding – especially if Ishie, the golden girl, was involved.

But Wilf knew he was kidding himself. If the police found Crog, his DNA would be everywhere. They'd nab him in no time. Either that or he'd be out in the wild, living off squashed squirrels till he died. And what was it all for?

A bowl. A beautiful bowl.

Well, if he couldn't have the bowl, he could at least get that little splinter of wood. Crog had it somewhere on him, didn't he?

Where would he have put it? In his mouth? Probably not, thought Wilf with relief. For Crog had said that he was afraid of choking and didn't like to sleep with it in his mouth. And this was a sleep, wasn't it? The very longest of sleeps.

Where else? Wilf got to his knees and felt in the many pockets of the photographer's waistcoat. Crog's skin, he noticed, was changing, becoming more yellowish, with a slightly greasy film. A cheese-and-onion crisp complexion.

There was nothing in the pockets. Wilf knew he shouldn't have bothered: it was too obvious. Thieves were always good at hiding things – that was half the art, wasn't it? So the piece of wood would not be in any expected place.

Maybe in his hair? The idea of combing his fingers through a corpse's hair was not appealing.

Wilf sat back and looked at Crog, lying with his head propped up against the tree trunk, one eye oddly at half mast and the rope dangling down his front – as if it was a part of him really. Well, it *was* part of him.

The rope. Of course!

Wilf picked up one end; it was still sodden and heavy. He tried to separate the strands, but the twine was swollen with damp and he could get no purchase. He tried again further up, nearer the knot. But still he couldn't prise the threads apart.

The solution came to Wilf suddenly, and he smiled at the simplicity of it. The rope, at the moment, was closed, secretly snibbed shut like one of those clever Japanese boxes. All he had to do was open it. He put one hand on either side of the knot and gave a hard, sharp twist. The folds of the rope separated, and there, shining wetly, was the splinter of wood, *his* splinter of wood. He hooked it out, and as his fingers closed around it, voices drifted into his mind like wisps of fog.

Then came another voice, familiar and accusing.

'What did you do that for?' Ishbel was standing directly behind him, in his shadow.

Guiltily he dropped the rope. 'Ishie! You gave me such a shock! How long have you been here?' He quickly slid the piece of wood into his back pocket.

'Long enough. You're losing your touch, letting me sneak up on you like that. I thought you said you'd call if you found him?'

'Crog's dead,' said Wilf.

'No! *No!*' Ishbel pushed past Wilf and stooped over the body. 'What happened? What did you do to him?'

'Nothing!' protested Wilf. 'Why do you always have to blame me? Remember how he was looking so peaky – I mean peakier than he normally does. I got here, and he just said it was time to go, and then, well, then he just went and died. I think he'd slunk off to do it away from us. Without the bowl, he didn't really have a reason to be here.'

'Poor old Crog,' sighed Ishbel. She stroked the hair off his forehead and then wiped her hands on her jeans. She peered down at the white oval of his face. She said slowly and wonderingly, 'If we were in hospital, what do you think they'd put as the cause of death?'

'I dunno. Disappointment?' Wilf shrugged.

'You don't die of disappointment,' she said. 'Or of too many chips. Vitamin deficiency might have been a possibility – but then he'd have been dead and gone years ago.' She shone the torch at Wilf. 'What *exactly* did you do?'

'Nothing!'

'Hmm. You've got that shifty look again . . . I know! You've taken something from him, haven't you?'

Normally Wilf would have denied it. But he felt tired. And the voices were murmuring in some distant part of his mind.

'That little bit of wood . . . It was for his own good really – he couldn't be forever trying to get that bowl back. He might die, but he wouldn't *rest*. There's a world of difference between the two.'

'Well, that sounds very virtuous, doesn't it?' said Ishbel sarcastically. 'Very good of you!'

'It *was* very good of me,' replied Wilf defiantly. 'I was doing him a favour.'

'No, Wilf. You nicked it. You stole from the dead. That's a new low – even for you.'

'It was *my* bowl!'

'You mean you stole it first?'

'And now he can sleep. He can die *properly*!' said Wilf.

'You're still gagging to get your hands on that bowl, aren't you. You'll end up like Crog.'

'No I won't. And stop preaching at me! You think you're so perfect,' said Wilf bitterly.

'I'm not even going to dignify that with a reply,' said Ishbel.

'Then *don't*! And just shut up!'

It was too dark to see, but Wilf knew she'd be rolling her eyes. Why, he wondered sadly, couldn't they ever stop bickering?

After a while Ishbel spoke again, but in a quite different tone. She said, 'What are we going to do with his body, anyway?'

What *did* you do with dead bodies? Wilf was at a loss. This was one of those ancient life skills that Crog would surely have had.

'We should really lay him on his back,' he said firmly.

They turned poor Crog's body round, and put his arms down by his side. Ishbel found two 50p coins in her purse and placed them on his eyelids.

'I don't know quite why I'm doing this,' she said. 'It makes him look like one of those old women in a beauty spa with slices of cucumber over their eyes.'

The coins glowed faintly in the torchlight. New metal eyes for Crog.

Wilf said, 'Let's get him sorted. I don't want to hang around here any longer.'

They carried out Crog's last wish, gathering up armfuls of dead leaves and laying them over his body. Ishbel wept as she worked.

'Don't cry,' said Wilf. 'He had to go back.'

'At least I could have given him something,' she sobbed.

'Like what? Conditioner? Hair serum?'

'Can't you ever be serious?' Ishbel paused. 'Maybe fudge. He did so love fudge.'

'Great!' said Wilf. 'So he'd be wincing all the way to the afterlife.'

She gave a snuffly laugh.

They worked on steadily through the night, and as the pile of leaves grew, they shored up the sides with branches. Eventually, when the mound was waist-high, it seemed right to stop, and Ishbel placed a small bunch of bluebells on the top.

'So what do we do now?' said Wilf.

'We need to go back to the shore,' replied Ishbel.

'Why?'

'I've got something still to do. You'll see!' She smiled.

They reached the road as dawn was turning the sky a gummy pink. High overhead a hawk wheeled. 'Did we drop some chips?' wondered Wilf. Then he remembered that birds of prey ate carrion, and that was what Crog was now.

They passed the sleeping village, and followed their previous route round the backs of the houses and down to the shore.

The estuary was calm now – just a faint ripple where only a few hours before the water had churned and foamed. Wilf stood on the tide line and cupped his hands. The water tasted faintly salty, but he didn't mind. He drank a little more – if he was banged up, it would be an age before he drank real, proper water that wasn't from a tap. He doused his face and neck, shaking off the drops like a dog.

The hills opposite were covered in blackened gorse and heather. Beyond were the rocks and the cave – and the terrible underwater tunnel. Wilf thought, *If death is anything like that tunnel, then God help Crog.*

He turned his gaze westwards. Three police cars were winding down the last stretch of coast road towards the bridge.

'It'll be that woman who gave us a lift yesterday,' said Ishbel, coming up beside him.

'She knew there was something not right about us,' agreed Wilf. 'Must've just got that feeling, mustn't she?'

'Must've just got that smell too,' said Ishbel. 'Proper Duke of Edinburgh people brush their teeth.'

Wilf noticed a smooth grey pebble dangling from Ishbel's hand, a piece of twine tied around its middle. 'What's that?'

'Ha!' Ishbel unclasped her fist and showed him. Tied to the twine in a neat, tight knot was the black triangle of wood.

'Hey! You took that from my pocket!' said Wilf.

'As I said, you're losing your touch.'

'Give us it,' he said, reaching for the piece of wood.

Ishbel quickly closed her fist again.

Wilf grabbed her hand. 'Hey! You stole that!' He said it jovially, but he was forcing her fingers apart.

She pulled herself free. 'And you stole it too,' she said. 'We've got to throw it back.'

'Why? We can keep it. It's my . . . my souvenir.'

'Your *souvenir*!' said Ishbel scornfully. 'Have you learned nothing in the last week?'

'What do you mean?' He was offended. 'I've learned loads. I can now catch a squirrel. I can row like a demon. I can make a soup out of wild mushrooms. That's more than you. You just got ill.'

'Yeah, but *really* learned,' she said. 'The important stuff.'

'Like what?' Out of the corner of his eye Wilf saw the last of the police cars stop on the bridge. The other two had driven on into the village. In a couple of minutes they'd be down on the shore.

'Like not holding onto things that aren't yours,' said Ishbel.

'It *is* mine!'

'No it isn't. That piece of wood doesn't belong to you . . . And it won't do you any good.'

'It's all right for you,' said Wilf. 'You never held the bowl. You don't know what it's like to want things.'

'You want too much. You always have done,' said Ishbel. 'I felt the bowl's power, and I stayed away. I made the decision, Wilf. You went the other way. Now you have to let it go. Not just the bowl, but that little bit of it too.'

'But it's tiny!'

'That doesn't matter. It's still part of the bowl.'

'We don't have to hold onto it,' Wilf said craftily. 'Give it to me and we can bury it instead.'

She looked at him in disbelief. 'You can't think I'm *that* stupid.'

'We bury it. *Finito!*' he said with a shrug. 'What's your problem?'

'Firstly you'd never bury it – you'd somehow sneak away with it. And if – *if* – you buried it, then you'd come back for it, wouldn't you? Or you'd always *think* about coming back for it. It would always be there.'

'I can give up that bit of wood any time I want,' said Wilf.

'So speaks the addict,' retorted Ishbel.

On the bridge the police driver was talking into his radio. Wilf didn't have long. Not long at all.

'Give it me!' he said.

'No!'

He made a grab for Ishbel's fist, but she was too quick for him and jumped backwards into the water.

That move was a mistake – now she was knee-high in the estuary and the water would slow her down. Wilf couldn't stop the ugly smile that spread across his face. She was his now, wasn't she? He took a step towards her, gimlet-eyed, ready for the tackle. He thought, *Nothing can save her now.*

'Give us it!' he said.

'For God's sake, Wilf!' cried Ishbel. 'What's got into you?' She stepped back. 'I'm not frightened, Wilf . . .'

But he knew better: she *was* frightened.

Ishbel lifted her arm to throw the pebble, and in that instant he lunged, toppling them both over. He wasn't aware of the freezing water or the stony sea bottom under his knees; he just grappled desperately. He nearly got to her hand, but she was quick as a fish and wriggled free. He grabbed her shoulder, but lost his hold when she kicked him in the stomach. The pain only made him angrier. She wasn't going to slip away!

He was pulling at her top and grabbing her hair. Now he was holding her tight around the throat, her eyes bulging. He was pressing her neck down. Down, down . . . Just a little more and her head would be under.

'Wilf!' she croaked. 'For God's sake! I'm your sister!'

Startled, he came back to himself. As if his hands were burning, he let go of her.

Ishbel sat up, holding her throat, coughing and spluttering horribly.

'Sorry,' he said uselessly. She was still coughing. He put a soaking wet arm round her shoulder, and rested it there like a dead dog. She shook him off.

Further up the shore, by the bins, the two police cars were drawing up.

'Sorry,' he said again. 'I don't know what got into me.'

But he *did* know, and so did she.

'Give it up, Wilf,' said Ishbel. 'You can't spend your life with the dead.'

He saw, to his horror, the red smudges on her neck

where his fingers had pressed down. If he'd held on any longer, if he'd got her head under the water . . . How had it come to this? He'd nearly killed his own sister. And all for a little splinter of wood that would have been a ticket to eternal misery.

'I'm sorry, Ishie,' he murmured.

'*Show* me you're sorry.' She held out the pebble with its twine and wood. He wanted that little piece of wood so badly he had to look away.

'Take it,' she said.

'You do it,' he said weakly. 'I can't trust myself.'

'No!' insisted Ishbel. '*You* do it. You stole the bowl, so you return it.'

Wilf reached out and took the pebble. It seemed to sing in his hand.

He didn't look down. He kept his fist closed. This was, he knew, like jumping off the highest diving board. A moment of pure, thoughtless determination.

Ishbel was watching him. What did he need? He was here with the silvery salt morning air and the sea and the hills at his feet. He had her. He had his whole life in front of him. And now was his moment.

He took a deep breath and ran out into the estuary, his arm raised above him. With a shout, he flung the pebble far up into the sky; it flew with its zigzag tail of twine and wood, made an arc through the air and finally dropped silently into the water. As it did so, a silver Mercedes roared across the bridge and was gone.

Wilf looked out over the surface of the water – the hole made by the pebble had sealed over immediately. *That*, he thought, *is how the past should be: clear and closed, a current running under and around you, but never pulling you down.*

He splashed his way back towards Ishbel. Up by the bins the police were getting out of their cars. It was, he realized to his surprise, a relief that all of the bowl was gone.

Ishbel laughed at him. 'That's a first for you, isn't it? Giving something back . . .'

'Yup, never knowingly returned stolen goods,' Wilf said cheerily.

He felt lighter now. There were no sounds, no voices. He took her hand, and calmly they walked up the beach towards the police cars.

ACKNOWLEDGEMENTS

I have so many people to thank. Denise Johnstone-Burt encouraged me at the very beginning and Laura Marshall and my sister-in-law Aideen walked Glencoe with me. My brother Neil advised on Gaelic and Scottish topography. My sister Harriet and my writer friends, Christine Purkis, Rebecca Lisle, Tracy Moyle-Maton and Shosh Copley, all read early drafts. My husband Jeremy provided huge amounts of moral support.

My agent Philippa Milnes–Smith at LAW gave me, as always, wonderful advice. And the team at Random House, in particular Natalie Doherty and Sophie Nelson, saw what *Crog* could be and bashed it into shape. I am hugely grateful to you all.